BRAVE THE WILD TRAIL

by Milly Howard

Bob Jones University Press, Greenville, South Carolina 29614

Brave the Wild Trail

Edited by Carolyn Cooper and Ruth Miller

Cover and illustrations by Tom Halverson

©1987 by Bob Jones University Press
Greenville, South Carolina 29614

ISBN 0-89084-384-8
Printed in the United States of America

20   19   18   17   16   15   14   13   12   11   10   9

To the Markos family
forever friends

Publisher's Note

Armed with the eighteen-foot bullwhips that earned them the name of "Crackers," the men on the Florida frontier wrestled their livelihoods from the wild scrub and marshlands where they had settled their families. Eben Bramlett was one of many drafted into the "Cow Cavalry" that had run cattle for the Confederacy's food supply during the Civil War. Now that the war is over and he is free to make his own way, he faces not only the wilderness but also a land that has become poverty-stricken because of the war.

The cattle in the scrub are still plentiful. Eben Bramlett's dream is to drive them down along the Kissimmee River to the southern coast. His twelve-year-old son Josh, also expert with both horse and bullwhip, is his partner. Together they assemble a small company to begin the four-month trip to Punta Rassa. In spite of rustlers, outlaws, and wolves ahead on the trail, they mount up and ride out.

The Bramletts face the dangers and difficulties on the trail with more than just their bullwhips or Eben's shotgun. For them, relying on the Lord through the hard times is a way of life. In many ways, Eben Bramlett typifies the American frontiersman, who went forward with his Bible and his tools into the wilderness.

Designed for middle school and junior high school children, *Brave the Wild Trail* is a book of high adventure sure to capture the reader's imagination. With a historical setting familiar to very few people, it opens up a new perspective for readers who enjoy frontier stories.

Contents

Chapter One
Gator Hole

The long canoe drifted lightly, hardly rippling the surface of the brackish water. A muscular man of medium height sat in the stern. The features of the boy at the bow resembled the man enough that the boy could be easily recognized as his son. In front of both, dripping paddles lay crosswise.

On either side of them, swamp maples and sweet gum trees stretched bare limbs to a pale February sky, and the knobby knees of cypress trees buckled above the water as if any minute the big trees would scramble out of their cold bath. The boy shivered. The swamp in winter was a dark and cold place.

"Josh."

The boy turned his head. He saw his father lift the shotgun and knew that their next alligator hole was just ahead. The canoe slipped silently under thickly hanging Spanish moss as they approached their deadly prey. The stream widened and revealed a bowl-shaped pool. The underbrush shrank back along both banks, allowing sunlight to pour down into the bowl. A heron stood on one leg in shallow water near the edge, preening itself. Two snakebirds craned their necks and pecked the air nervously as the canoe approached. Turning his head, Josh saw the sand spit jutting out from the left bank. Alligators stretched out on the narrow spit, seeking the feeble warmth from the sun.

Eben Bramlett moved quietly. He aimed the gun at the nearest alligator and squeezed the trigger. The swamp exploded in a clamor of noise and action. Alligators slid off the sand and back into the deeper water of the pool. The heron and snakebirds lifted off, their screeching almost drowned by the beating whir of thousands of blackbirds taking wing from the brush.

Josh and his father pulled the canoe onto the spit of sand a safe distance from the fallen alligator. They waited until the clamor subsided and quiet settled back over the swamp. Then Eben handed the shotgun to his son, warning him, "If he moves, blow his head off."

Josh steadied the gun against a fallen palmetto. His finger tightened on the trigger as he watched his father's slow progress along the spit. Though they had been repeating this routine all afternoon, tension caused sweat to bead along his hairline and trickle slowly down the side of his nose.

Taking care to stay out of the line of fire, Eben approached the lone alligator that remained on the spit, sprawled half in, half out of the water. He kicked sand toward the motionless beast, expecting the warning hiss of a live gator. It didn't move. Edging closer, Eben prodded it with a long piece of deadwood. Still, the gator didn't respond. Eben called back to Josh. "Reckon he's down for good."

Josh eased his cramped muscles and stood, flexing his fingers. His bare feet scuffed the warm sand as he joined his father. "We gonna skin him here?"

Eben's gray eyes measured the angle of the sun. "It's getting late, and I know your ma's fretting. He's a little 'un. I doubt if he runs five feet. Let's take him home."

There were already a couple of fresh hides in the canoe. They levered the gator into the vessel, where it sprawled bonelessly on top of the pile in the middle section. Eben grunted in satisfaction. "At two dollars a hide, we'll have money in the cash box. We're gettin' there, Josh, little by little."

"Do we have enough to get a dog, too, Pa?" Josh asked eagerly as he climbed in, splashing water.

Eben shoved the canoe off the spit and leaped in, moving lightly for a man of his build. He glanced back at the boy. "Lord willing," he replied, picking up a paddle. "Depends on prices. They've been up and down so much since Lee signed at Appomattox that a body has trouble knowing just what things'll cost."

For a while, man and boy didn't speak, but bent to their paddles. They headed out of the marsh, sliding underneath the moss-shrouded trees that crowded along the banks of the dark creek.

Near the inlet where the creek flowed into the St. Johns, Eben stood to pole across the shallows. Crawdads scurried as he thrust the long paddle into their midst. Josh lifted his paddle, listening to a faint slithering sound that echoed the movement of the crabs. At first he thought the sound was sand raking across the bottom of the canoe. Then a sudden movement in the bottom of the canoe gave him an instant's warning.

"He's alive!"

Without hesitation, both Eben and Josh leaped out and charged across the sandbar to the bank. In the same moment, a sideways swipe of gator tail exploded the deserted canoe into chunks of splintered wood. A spray of salt water and wood fragments showered the inlet as the gator flipped with the force of his blow and plunged into deeper water.

"You blackwater monster! You—you—" Shaking with fear and rage, Eben yelled, "Gator!"

He caught Josh's hand and hauled him up on the bank. "Every time we bring one of them beasts in, I never know whether to set you by the head or the tail of those critters. There's no knowin' which end's the worse."

Josh cleared his throat. "Well, he missed that time," he said shakily. "Most time they don't give any warning."

"The Lord sent you a warning by makin' it move first. I could've sworn it was dead." Eben scooped up a double handful of water and splashed it on his face. "If He didn't watch out for us out here, we wouldn't have much chance, would we?" Then, rubbing his hands on his wet overalls, he started through the shallows toward the floating hides. "You wait here. I'll salvage what I can."

Eben fished the few hides out of deep water and plunged back to the bank. The gun was wet, as were the shells, but it was there, thrown on the sandbar.

"Well, son, we've a long walk back into the scrub."

His eyes scanned the thick brush on both sides of the river. Carefully choosing his way, he pushed his shoulders through, easing the saw-toothed branches of the palmetto bushes to keep them from springing back across Josh's face.

By the time they reached the scrub, the setting sun had painted the lower edge of the sky a rich crimson. The two figures, one lean and wiry, the other thin and spindle-legged like a colt, moved faster into the approaching darkness. Before them, hammocks broke the evenness of the scrub, raising tall slash pine and palms to the sky. They veered north slightly, heading toward Yonder Hammock, a raised stand of pine and hardwood.

They reached the clearing as the moon rose above the big live oaks. The pale light softened the harsh edges of the small homestead the Bramletts had forged out of the backcountry Florida wilderness. It made dark latticework of the corral and holding pen and silhouetted the bulkier shapes of the cabin and the barn. Above the rough cabin, it silvered the thin stream of smoke that trickled upward into the darkening sky.

"Ma!" Josh broke into a run. "Ma!"

The door swung open and a small woman appeared in the lamplight that streamed across the porch. "I thought sure one of you was alligator bait," she said lightly, trying to ease the worry lines that creased her forehead.

Eben dropped the hides on the porch. "You were pretty nigh right this time," he said soberly. "We just took our last gator hide."

"What happened?"

"You should've seen that old gator, Ma," Josh said, sniffing at the smell coming from the iron pot on the fireplace coals. "It busted up that canoe good!"

He didn't hear the catch in his mother's voice. "The canoe?"

"You must've been praying awful hard today, Penny," Eben said. He gave his wife a reassuring hug. "One of the gators wasn't quite dead. If Josh hadn't—well, there'll be no more gator hides. There's got to be a better way to earn cash money to get the horses we need."

"Thank God," Penny Bramlett said fervently. She tucked straying wisps of coppery hair back into a restraining bun and reached for the iron pot. "You two sit. I know you're hungry."

When the poke greens had disappeared and only crumbs remained of the fried corncakes, Josh climbed the ladder to the small loft. He lay on his moss-stuffed mattress and listened sleepily to the settling-down sounds from below. He heard faint creaking noises and knew that Ma had finished the dishes and was sitting in the old rocker that she had insisted on bringing all the way from Georgia.

"I rocked Josh in that chair, and I imagine I'll be rocking his brothers and sisters in the same chair," she had told Eben. But there had been no others. At twelve, Josh was the only child born to Eben and Penny Bramlett. He had grown up alone, with only his parents for company. In fact, for a long time there had been only Penny for company, during the months when Eben was driving cattle for Jacob Summerlin's "Cow Cavalry" during the Civil War. Life in the scrub could have been lonely, but Penny went out of her way to make things enjoyable. And now Eben treated Josh like a partner as well as a son. Josh had his parents, and he had an occasional raccoon or red fox for a pet.

For years, that had been enough. Then one day a rare visitor had passed through the hammock with a brace of hunting dogs. He left Penny the huge conch shell he had used as a hunting horn and left Josh with the love of dogs. From that time on, Josh dreamed of owning a dog— a pet that would be his own, to stay with him forever and never seek freedom as the wild animals had done.

Just wait, he thought, thinking of the empty holding pen. *Those old gator hides will get us enough cash money for horses. Then we'll round up brush cows and drive them to sell, just like Pa said we would. We're gonna have us a cattle ranch yet.*

Groggily, Josh heard the familiar clink as the cash box was opened. Pa would be counting up their money, planning a trip to town. *And there'll be enough left over for a dog,* Josh thought as his eyelids closed. *I just know it. I got to get a dog. I just got to.*

Chapter Two
Matlock's Landing

"Wake up, Josh."

Josh opened his eyes. Night still shadowed the loft. He rolled over and let his eyelids close again.

This time the unseen voice was more insistent. "Wake up, partner. It's time for some trading."

Trading! Josh sat up, fully awake. Pa was going to the trading post today! Today he'd get a horse and maybe, just maybe, a dog!

He rolled off the mattress and scrambled for his shirt and britches. "Coming, Pa!"

Eben was waiting at the foot of the ladder. "Me and your ma decided it was time to get on with the cattle business, partner. Reckon there might be some horses at the post near Kissimmee. Figure a cowboy ought to pick out his own horse, don't you?"

"Yessir!" All sleep had been wiped from Josh's wide eyes. He combed his sandy hair with his fingers and took his place at the table.

Ma didn't turn from the fireplace. "Wash first."

"Aww," Josh groaned and hurried outside to splash water over his hands and face. When he got back, the plates held scrambled eggs and biscuits. Wild blackberry tea sent curling steam from the cups.

"Coffee would sure hit the spot," Eben said wistfully, breaking open one of Ma's steaming biscuits. "And butter. Maybe there'll be a little change left over after we make our purchases. You thought about what we need, Pen?"

"Just about everything," Ma replied. She didn't say it had been a hard year. She didn't have to. "I'm about out of flour. We need salt, some meal, and a few other things. And coffee, of course. I made a list." She patted the pocket of her huge apron.

"We'll get what we can," Eben promised. When breakfast was over, he stood up. "Okay, Josh. How about harnessing Ornery while I load the hides?"

"Sure, Pa."

It didn't take long to hitch the big ox to the wagon and load it with the hides Eben and Josh had taken over the last few months. They were ready when Ma closed the cabin door.

"What's that jingling sound, woman?" Eben teased as he helped her onto the wagon seat. "Don't tell me you have our life savings in that purse?"

"Every penny we have, Eben Bramlett," she laughed, shaking the purse gently. "And I'm itching to spend."

Josh leaned back and laughed happily. It always pleased him when his parents teased each other, and today was full to the brim with all the happiness he could hold. The golden mist of early sunrise couldn't match the glow that warmed his insides. It was going to be a grand day.

Eben felt it too. Josh could tell by the sparkle in his gray eyes and the way he repeatedly cracked the eighteen-foot bullwhip in the air. Josh let out a full yodel to match the pistol cracks of the whips.

Penny laughed outright. "You two'll scare away every bit of game between here and Kissimmee. And Ornery'll not go one whit faster for all the noise you can make."

Grinning sheepishly, the two subsided, knowing she was right. Ornery plodded along at his usual snail's pace. Josh's tongue far outdid the ox's pace, for he chattered along a mile a minute. Eben and Penny were hard put to answer all his questions, but they tried, sharing secret smiles of pride at his curiosity.

Long before noon he was investigating the contents of the lunch basket Penny had packed before dawn. She slapped his hands lightly to keep him from scrambling the food. She pulled out strips of dried jerky for him to chew on. "This'll keep the wolf away until time to eat," she said.

Josh gnawed on the strip, feeling his stomach contract in anticipation. "What else is in the basket, Ma?" he asked.

"Biscuits and some dewberry jam I put up last spring," she answered. "It'll keep until Pa gets us a rabbit."

Josh sighed. Noon seemed a long time away. He tired of the expanses of brown grass and lay back in the wagon, watching the sky. It was blue with the promise of early spring. High above, thick clouds towered, layer upon layer of white cotton, warm with the radiance of the sun. For a while, he picked out shapes in the clouds. Then he half-dozed, off and on, dreaming about his dog.

The ground leveled out near Kissimmee, and the wagon jolted along on cattle trails through thick grass. Occasionally they could see herds of wild cattle grazing in the distance.

Eben pointed them out. "That's what I want, Pen," he told his wife. "What worries me, though, is the weight the steers lose on a drive. The cattle we drove for Summerlin during the war lost between one-fifty and two hundred pounds apiece before we got them to Georgia. And they were good grass-fed steers. The poor yellowhammers we're gonna pop out of the scrub will be walking skeletons before we get them to market."

"If there's a way, you'll find it, Eben." Ma smiled up at him.

Josh stirred out of his lethargy to watch the cattle. Most ignored the presence of the slow-moving wagon. Others bunched together and galloped away, tails flicking as they ran.

"They're purty," he observed. "Leastways, they're purtier than the cows around Yonder. How come, Pa?"

Eben pointed with the folded whip. "In a few weeks all this will be a sea of green," he told Josh. "Not a brown blade of grass will be left. It's like God renews the whole of Floridy, greening it up just for His own pleasure."

"It gets green around our place too," Josh replied. "How come the cows are so scrawny?"

"We don't have the grass that's here. This is good prairie grass. Cows grow fat on it."

Josh grew tired of watching the distant cows. He leaned closer and said, "Ma, Pa has his dream about our cattle ranch, and I have mine about my dog. Do you have a dream?"

Penny thought for a moment. Then she said shyly, "I'd like to have some orange trees."

"Orange trees? Like those we saw at Fort Drum?" Eben asked.

Penny nodded. "They were like clouds caught on thick stems, Josh. And the perfume, why, it was sweeter than any a woman might want. If I had a few of those trees outside my kitchen door, I'd be right proud."

"Then you'll have them," Eben said firmly. "Be our first purchase with the money from the cows."

When they stopped to eat in the filtered shade of a palm grove, Penny took the picnic basket down, and Josh followed his father into the grass. Eben moved quietly and carefully, until he came within sight of a rabbit run. He held the whip loosely in his hand and waited. Pretty soon, a long-eared jack came hopping by, eyes alert for danger. It didn't pay much regard to the man and boy, who were holding perfectly still. As though uneasy, it turned its head slightly. Pa's arm flicked; the whip sang out like a snake striking. There was a crack of the lash, and the rabbit tumbled over. Eben went forward to collect it. Josh helped him skin it, and they took it back to the wagon.

After they had finished their meal, Eben stood and stretched. He pointed out trails of blue on the horizon. "Smoke," he told them. "Cattlemen are burning off the underbrush. New grass will grow in its place."

Early afternoon brought them closer to the thin line of blue. The smell of burning wood lay heavy on the air. Josh abandoned all notions of taking a nap and lay, propped against the side of the wagon, watching the fire. "Will we go through it, Pa?"

"I hope not, but folks don't have much sense about fire." Eben flicked Ornery with the whip. "Fire can get out of control too easy."

Penny gave him a worried look but said nothing. They rolled through a sandy stretch of blackened pines. The fire had passed through the trees and left them twisted and scarred. Josh stood, holding onto the wagon seat, in order to see better. A deathly quiet hung over trees, as thick as the smoke that still rose from the burned trunks.

"Look," Josh said quietly, pointing to a tree trunk that still burned with a slow, hot fire.

"It's heart of pine," Eben said. "It'll burn for days, slow like that. At night, it'll glow like torchlight."

"And over there, Eben?" Penny pointed to tiny flickers of flame half-hidden under black smoke.

"Burning muck," Eben replied soberly. "I've seen fires like that go on for weeks, sometimes months. They're burning from underground."

Penny shuddered. "It reminds me of what the Good Book says about hell. Let's get out of here, Eben."

The bullwhip cracked and stung, cracked and stung. For once Ornery got the message. The wagon wheels began to roll faster.

The smoke had faded to a dull haze as they reached the trading post. Built of cochina rock and palm logs, it sprawled under the shade of live oak trees near the slow-moving Kissimmee River. Behind it was a log barn and a small corral that held about a dozen animals. As soon as he saw them, Josh whooped and leaped off the wagon.

"Hold on, Josh!" Penny called in alarm as he disappeared around the corner of the trading post.

"Let the boy go, Pen," Eben told her. "He'll come to no harm here." He hitched the ox to the post and helped Penny off the wagon. She stepped thankfully onto the shaded porch, glad to get out of the hot afternoon sun. Slipping her bonnet off her head, she fanned herself gently and stopped by the handrail to look at the river.

"It's so pretty here, Eben," she said softly. "Come and look."

Below them, chickens scratched at the bare ground under the widespread branches of the live oaks. A few yards away the ground sloped gently toward the river. Coots dived near the reedy bank, setting up a raucous clamor as they dived for minnows.

"It's as pretty as a picture. See, the hanging moss makes a frame for the whole scene."

Eben grinned. "Thought you were tired of the moss."

"It's a mess, for sure." Penny sniffed. "But I never said it wasn't pretty."

"Well, come on in," Eben said, touching her elbow. "Let's see what else you find pretty."

Inside, Penny stopped to survey the shelves with dismay. Trips to the post came seldom, for cash money had been scarce during the war and, too, provisions at the post had been slim. They weren't much better now. Hesitantly, she fingered the list folded in her pocket.

Ben Matlock came out of a back room, scratching his thick black beard. "Hello, folks," he said. "What can I do for you?"

"Got some hides," Eben replied. "They're on the wagon."

"Coon, gator, or skunk?"

"Gator," Eben replied, leading the older man out the door. "And some coon hides that my boy cured. This'll be the last of the gator hides, though. The one that got away almost took me and my boy with it."

"Yeah. One of the Latrell boys tangled with a sixteen-footer last week and came out short a foot himself. Near died in the process. Skunk hides are safer. Running two dollars a pelt, same as gator. How about bringing some next trip?"

"Nope. I came face to face with one skunk last year. Had to sleep in the barn for a week. Ruint my clothes. Two dollars is right cheap for skunk."

The trader grinned. "Seems that's the way most folks feel. Though there's some that would do anything for money. A lot of strange folks have been in and out here since the war ended. A pack rode in the other day that near froze my blood. You see or hear anything unusual out in the scrub?"

"Not much," Eben replied soberly. "We're a long way out."

"Well, keep an eye peeled. I wouldn't put anything past that bunch. Now, how many hides you got here?"

"Fifteen gator and twenty coon. I was aiming for more before coming in, but I didn't make it."

The trader fingered the hides, looking for bullet holes. He grunted, then turned his head to spit. "Looks like you got yourself thirty-five dollars, anyhow. You aiming to take it in cash or trade?"

Before Eben could answer, Josh raced around the corner, calling, "Pa! Pa!" He halted beside his father, breathing quickly. When he saw the trader, he pushed back the hair that had fallen over his eyes and waited, every muscle tensed with excitement.

"This is Josh, my son," Eben said, a slow smile warming his face. "I guess he found his horse."

"Well, if horses be your need, you came to the right place," the trader said. He started back to the corral, motioning them to follow. "Which one did you fancy, boy?"

"I'll show you."

Josh hooked his arms over the top rail and waited. In the corral, three big cavalry horses moved about easily. Behind them, bunched in a corner, five small horses stood silently. The dust that dulled their coats didn't hide their protruding ribs.

"That one." Josh pointed to one of the smaller horses. It was black as night and thin as a panther. Eben raised his eyebrows. "It sure looks like it went through the same winter we did, Josh. And those poor bones aren't likely to fatten up in the scrub. Now, take a look at those big horses. Those animals look to be in fine condition."

The light went out of Josh's face. He turned politely to look at the larger horses.

"Traded those from some Reb cavalry officers on the way home after the war," the trader said. "Good horses."

"How much?" Eben asked.

"Twenty apiece."

Eben shook his head. "That's high."

"Good horseflesh's hard to come by. Wolves got most of the spring colts last year. It's a fair price."

"I reckon. Trouble is, I need two. And supplies."

"Well, the little 'uns come cheap. Just got them in last week. No time to fatten them up yet."

"How much?" Eben asked resignedly.

"Let you have two for twenty. They're stronger than they look, and they're used to living in the scrub. Fella' who sold them to me said he took them off some Seminoles."

"Well, let's look at them," Eben said. Josh was off the rail and inside the corral before his father reached the gate. He headed for the black horse.

While Josh murmured and stroked the small horse, Eben checked the others carefully. "At least they're not wild," he said, still doubtful.

"Nope. Well-trained, I bet. Those Injuns are good with horses. But don't think I'm rushing you into anything." Ben ran his big hands over the flank of a spotted brown horse. "Sooner or later, some cowboy'll ride in here looking to buy 'em."

"Cowboy?" Eben's head came up.

The trader nodded. "Injuns used them to run cattle. Best little cow horses around."

Eben's mood lightened. "Well, that's what we need them for. We'll take this one and the black."

Josh's grin threatened to split his face. "Can I have the black, Pa? Can I?"

"Sure," Eben replied. "Why don't you get them ready while I settle up?"

"Okay, Pa."

Josh led the two horses to the barn while Ben and Eben headed for the post. "Good boy you have there," the older man said. "Guess he's a help to you, out back so far. Only one?"

Eben nodded. "He gets along okay, but I'd like to see the boy get a dog. A catch dog that'd work the cattle and still be a companion to the boy. Know of any for sale?"

Ben shook his huge head. "Not right off. I'll keep an eye out. Maybe next trip."

Eben sighed. "The boy was counting on a dog."

hide

"Looks like that black horse might make up for a little disappointment over the dog," Ben said, grinning. "I never seen a boy take to a horse like that one."

"Maybe so."

Eben found Penny in the store, poring over her list. "Got what you need?" he asked, mentally trying to calculate the cost of horses, tack, and other supplies. He gave up and came to look over her shoulder. "We need all that?"

"Don't fret," Penny said slowly. "They don't seem to have some of it anyways. The war left this land poorer in more ways than one."

Ben plumped a sack of flour down on the counter. "Yer right," he said, black eyes somber. "Steamboats didn't bring much this time. Leastways, we're not as bad off as folks up in Georgia."

Eben nodded. He had seen the hunger on the cattle drives to the Georgia line. Folks had lined the river to watch the cattle swim over. Once, the current had drowned two cows. He had watched in amazement as people crowded into the river, dragging the carcasses to shore. Knives had flashed as the meat was eagerly divided. It had been over in minutes, but the sight had stayed with Eben ever since.

"We aren't hungry. Game's plentiful."

Ben reached behind him. "What we do have plenty of is shot and shells. Like a feast after a famine, so t'speak."

Eben inspected the store eagerly. The whip had provided a constant supply of small game for their table, but the shot would bring down deer, maybe even bear. He selected what he needed and added it to Penny's supplies. When the total was tallied, he handed the cash over ruefully. "Down to bare bones again, Pen."

"Cash money's no good if it don't buy what we need, anyways," Penny said reassuringly. "We got enough."

Josh came in. "Come see the horses, Ma," he said eagerly. "I got them tied to the back of the wagon. Mine's black as the middle of night. That's why I named her Midnight."

He turned to his father. "Did you find a dog, Pa?"

"Looks like we all run into a little disappointment," Eben said slowly. "Don't seem to be any dogs available right now."

Josh struggled with his feelings, determined not to let them show in front of the big trader. He looked up. "Iff'n you find one, could you hold it for me?"

"Sure, son," Ben replied kindly. "I'll keep an eye out for a good 'un."

Chapter Three
Danger at Spaniard's Spring

"Pa?"

Eben prodded Ornery with the whip. "Yes, son?"

"How come the man took the horses away from the Seminoles? And if he stole them, how come we bought them?"

"I don't hold with what the man did, son," Eben replied thoughtfully, "but it was legal. The Seminoles lost the right to own cattle and horses before they were sent west."

"I thought that was a long time ago."

"Uh-huh. You were still in the cradle."

"Then how did the man get these horses?"

"Some of the Indians didn't want to go. They went deep into the Everglades where they hid from their hunters. They've been there all this time. Reckon, with the passin' of time, they felt a mite free to move about. They got caught."

Penny made a sharp sound.

"Ma?" Josh leaned forward. "What did you say?"

His mother's lips were tightly compressed, and a frown drew a thin line above her dark eyebrows.

Eben glanced at her. "By the time we got to Floridy, most of the Indian trouble was over. Me and your ma never were in the thick of it like some of the other settlers.

We'd only been in the scrub a year when Billy Bowlegs and his tribe were sent west. Most went with Billy, but, as I said before, some didn't. The government set a price on the Seminoles, and they were hunted down for bounty."

Penny's back set straight as a palm bole and her bonnet trembled. "Bounty placed on human beings, of all things! Women and children, too!"

"Why, Pa?"

"Well, I guess the government wanted to make sure the Indians were captured alive. They set the bounty hoping to avoid massacres." Eben cracked the whip, trying to force Ornery to quicken his shambling pace. The ox snorted. He slowed down and shook his head as if to dislodge a persistent blue fly. Eben sighed and settled back on the seat. "An ox is hardly better than a mule."

Josh leaned over the back of the wagon seat, resting his chin on his bony arms. "Did you know any bounty hunters, Pa?"

"You might say so." Eben grinned suddenly. "A couple of them tracked a young boy to our place. You were just toddling at the time. I had taken the stock to water. Your ma was alone, but she made short work of them. They left, slinking back into the scrub like curs with their tails between their legs."

"What on earth did you do, Ma?" Josh leaned forward, surprised at the sudden pink that brightened her cheeks.

Penny set her lips primly. "I was foolish, son. I let my anger trap me into endangering your life and my own. If your pa hadn't come back when he did—"

"She'd have fried them both for supper." Eben laughed out loud. "As it was, the young Indian went on his way, well fed. And we never saw hide nor hair of the other two again." He chuckled, glancing sideways at Penny. "Just remember son, an iron cooking pot can be a deadly weapon in the hands of an angry woman."

"Pshaw," Penny said softly, settling the bonnet firmly and swaying as the wagon churned slowly through the sand. "A body does what's needed."

"Did you ever see the Indian again?" Josh asked. "What did he look like? Were you scared?"

"Well, no. He never came back," Eben replied. "And he looked like most Seminoles, I guess. His shirt was half-torn off from hiding in the scrub, and his britches hadn't fared much better."

"I sure would like to see one," Josh said wistfully. "I've never seen a real Indian."

"You might sometime. I run into a few once in a while," his father replied, clucking at Ornery. "But they're not the ones I'm worried about right now. Ben Matlock said a group of men were roaming the backcountry, up to all sorts of mischief. He thinks they might be dangerous. I want both of you to be careful of strangers."

"Are they deserters from the war?"

"Could be. Could be escaped convicts from Georgia, too. There's not much law here, Josh. And even less in the scrub. There'll be stealin', rustlin', and all sorts of meanness flourishing until there is."

"Reckon when we get our herd goin', I'll need a gun," Josh said. "I'll blast any rustlers right out of their saddles."

His mother turned and stared. Eben laughed. "Whoa there, son. Let's take one step at a time. Besides, if your ma can defend herself with an iron pot, you can manage with the whip for a while."

"The good Lord is our protector, Josh," Penny reprimanded. "No harm will come to us."

"But Pa carries a gun," Josh protested. He leaned over his father's shoulder. "And he was in the war, too."

"Never had to shoot a man, son," Eben replied. "During the war, we drovers fought bad weather, wild steers, and wolves, but we never ran into any troops. The Lord kept us safe."

"But what if a man drawed down on you?"

"The bullwhip's just as good as a gun, most of the time. And most varmints'll let you alone if you don't bother them." He paused for a moment, then answered honestly. "But once in a while, when you come right up against a flat-bellied or a two-legged snake, a gun's mighty handy to have."

"You just pray it doesn't come to that," Penny said soberly. "And I don't want to hear any more talk of killin', Josh. Why don't you see to the horses?"

"Sure, Ma."

Josh clambered over the bags of flour and supplies and braced himself in the back corner of the wagon. Before they had left the trading post, the two small horses had been given a full feeding of oats. Now, tied to the back of the wagon, they walked along briskly, easily keeping up with the slow movement of the ox. The food might have perked them up, but it hadn't done much for their appearance. The sandy dust spun up by the wagon wheels covered their coats, making them appear more scraggly than ever.

Josh hung his legs over the back and talked to the horses, lavishing on Midnight all the love he had stored up for the dog. "I'd be riding you myself," he told the little horses, "if'n Pa wasn't worried about you throwing me off and running away, you being a new horse and all. You wouldn't though. I know. And when I get me a dog, we'll ride all over the scrub and back in a day."

He noticed the damp shine under the dust on their coats.

"Reckon they're thirsty, Pa?" Josh called back to his father.

"Reckon. I'm spittin' cotton myself. Spaniard's Spring is about two miles west of here." Using the folded end of the whip, Eben pointed toward a cypress head rearing like an island in the sea of brown grass and rustling palmettos. "We'll stay the night."

"That's Spaniard's Spring?" Josh shivered in spite of the warmth from the late afternoon sun. "Maybe we'll see the Spaniard's ghost, Pa. Or we'll find his gold. Can we look for it, Pa?"

"Now you know that's just somebody's old tale, made up to pass the time. Been any gold there, it would've been found a long time ago."

"It might be just waiting for the right person," Josh said dreamily. "I heard tell the Spaniard himself would pick the one to find the gold. They say he appears on the night of the silver moon to show the way."

"Now who's been filling your head with such nonsense?" Penny asked. "There's no such thing!"

Late in the afternoon the sun disappeared, and the sky turned gray. "There'll be a heavy dew tonight," Eben said. "Maybe a late frost. We'll have to sleep under the canvas."

"Pity we couldn't have made it all the way home," Penny replied. She shivered and pulled her shawl over her shoulders. "We'll catch our death of cold."

"We'll keep warm," Eben said. "I put the bearskins under the canvas. A good fire and hot food, then we'll cuddle up and be warm as three little bugs."

They reached the cypress hammock just before dusk. Mist had already begun to rise from the ground, shrouding the palmettos and curling pale fingers of fog across the sandy road. Josh crowded closer to the wagon seat as they passed under live oaks and cypress half-disguised by trailing Spanish moss. He peered into the sudden darkness, straining to see through the shadows. He listened so hard his ears tingled with the strain, but the spongy carpet of pine needles deadened even the clop-clop of Ornery's hooves and muffled the creaking of the wagon wheels.

"Pa?" Josh found himself whispering.

"Right here, Josh." His father's firm voice banished the strange shapes forming from the shadows. The road widened, and Eben halted the ox in a deserted clearing.

"Better gather deadwood before it gets too damp, Josh, but don't go far," he said. "I'll unhitch the ox and horses. When we're through, we'll find us a coon to fry."

Josh swung his legs over the side of the wagon and leaped to the ground in one easy movement. He gathered the firewood hastily, keeping close to the wagon and away from the surrounding underbrush. From time to time, he returned to the center of the clearing and dumped the branches on the dead ashes used by other travelers. Eben came to help after the ox and horses were secured in the remains of an old corral and water was brought up from the spring. He struck his flint and fanned the sparks. They caught on a lighter knot Josh had placed at the bottom of the pile, and flames leaped, licking greedily at the rest of the branches.

"That's good, son," Eben said, going to the wagon to get the bullwhip. "Now get a flambeau from the fire and let's get some fresh meat."

They left Penny at the fire, stirring batter for biscuits. A few yards under the trees, the light from the flambeau reflected two green sparks an inch or so apart. "Coon," Pa whispered in satisfaction. He uncoiled the whip. His arm flashed back, then forward and a sound like a shot shattered the quiet. The raccoon tumbled to their feet.

"Pa! Did you hear that?" Josh said. He was standing a few feet away, to the left.

"What, son?" Eben asked.

Josh peered into the darkness. He shivered, feeling the hairs prickle on the back of his neck. "It sounded like a moan."

"Might've been the coon." Eben scooped it up and turned. "Let's get it on the fire. I'm hungry enough to eat a bear."

He strode back toward the fire with Josh crowding on his heels. While Eben cleaned the raccoon, Josh went to the corral to talk to the horses. The horses were uneasy. They moved back and forth restlessly. From time to time, the black horse would lift its head and watch the boy, ears pricked.

"Don't tell me you know about the Spaniard, too," Josh whispered, chuckling at his own foolishness. He stroked the horse gently. "We're going to be friends. Just you wait and see."

When the coon was in the skillet, Josh returned to the fire. He burrowed a hollow into the sand as near to the flames as he could get without scorching his skin. Then he lay back, sleepily watching the sparks drift upward with the blue gray smoke. Out of the darkness a March wind sprang up, rustling the leaves of the trees and whispering through the ferns. It blew the murkiness out of the sky, leaving the clearing capped with a dark crystal, sparkling with tiny pinpoints of blue white fire. Josh breathed in the crispness of the night air, the dampness of wet leaves, and the woody scent of the smokefire. The warmth of family and well-being drove any lingering uneasiness back into the dark ring of trees. The sand cradled the tiredness from his thin body. Josh was besieged by a gnawing hunger long before the smell of hot biscuits and frying meat hung in the night air.

"Is it done yet, Ma?" he asked for the seventh time. When she gave him an exasperated slap with her wooden spoon, he dodged. "I can't help it, Ma," he said, grinning. "My stomach thinks my throat's been cut."

Eben joined them at the fire. "A growing boy needs his food," he said, ruffling Josh's hair. "Ain't we the ones, Josh. Not many can cook like your ma. I've never known anybody else to work miracles with less. Even when we've been down to cattail flour and wild berries, or gopher, or nothin' but poke greens, vittles have been right tasty."

Penny's hair glinted with firelight as she lifted the dutch oven from the coals. She tried unsuccessfully to hide her pleasure. "Go on with you now, both of you. You'd eat anything put on the table."

"Maybe and maybe not." Josh held out his plate. "I draw the line at rattlesnake. Ain't nothing I hate worse than a rattler."

"Better shake out the bedding good tonight, then," Eben warned. "These cold nights draw snakes to warmth like bees to flowers. A six-footer crawled into bed with me one night when I was bear hunting. Makes a body's skin fairly crawl to remember."

"Hush! Or I'll not sleep a wink tonight, wagon or not," Penny said quickly.

Josh shuddered in agreement. "I'll shake the skins out good, Ma."

"And I'll help," she promised. "Now eat up."

When the meal was finished and the fire was banked, they shook out the canvas and bearskins. Eben rearranged the supplies to form an open space in the center of the wagon. He tucked the package Penny had made of the remaining coon and biscuits at the bottom of the wagon and laid one bearskin fur-side up in the open space. Josh and Penny climbed in and covered themselves with the other, fur side down. Eben followed and pulled the canvas cover loosely over the top.

Sometime in the night Josh woke. For a moment, cocooned in the black fur, he forgot where he was. Then he remembered and lay still, listening to the quiet breathing of his parents and wondering uneasily about what had awakened him. Above him he could hear a slight crackle as the canvas moved in the breeze, and he knew that Pa had been right about the late frost. He turned his head slightly. Something was moving stealthily near his ankle. His breath froze, then came in jerky gasps. He forced himself to lie still.

"Pa," he whispered. The movement stopped, then jerked away quickly as if startled by the sound of his voice. Fear swept over him. "Pa! Pa!"

Eben woke instantly. He rolled over quickly, gun in hand. The canvas flipped up and back. A figure sprang away from the wagon wheel and leaped across the clearing. It stumbled and sprawled in the sand. In that moment, Eben was upon the figure. Josh heard a sharp, guttural cry. A snarling animal rushed out from under the circling trees. It leaped upon the struggling shadows, growling. Josh grabbed the bullwhip from the wagon and charged into the fray.

"Eben! Josh!" Penny called frantically, hurrying to throw branches on the fire. The branches caught, and light flared up. Josh saw his father struggling with a boy and a wild-looking dog.

"Call off the dog," Eben commanded, still holding the boy down. "We won't hurt you."

The boy made another strange sound, and the dog backed away. Hackles raised, it still rumbled menacingly. Eben stood up, keeping his movements slow and easy. The boy scrambled to his knees. He clutched the package of leftovers to his chest and glared up at Eben defiantly.

"If you be hungry," Eben said sternly, "you could have come to our fire. We would've shared our vittles."

The defiance faded into sullenness. "Most don't."

Josh stared at the dark face, the tangled hair, and the worn clothes. "Are you a Seminole?"

The boy didn't answer. He glanced back into the shadows, then looked at Eben. His inspection of the man was cautious but thorough.

Eben relaxed and released his hold on the gun. "You're welcome to what you have there. And there's more if you need it."

The boy stood up, facing them without fear. "I am Willie Tiger. I will pay you back, but I need the food now. I have no weapons to hunt with, and my grandfather is sick."

"Grandfather?" Penny moved forward. "Where is he?"

"Back there." The boy pointed to the shadows. "I don't know what is wrong with him. I think he's dying."

Penny gave an exclamation of concern. "Take us to him."

The boy paused a moment, then nodded and led the way through the brush to a spot near the tree where they had killed the coon. An old man lay in a bed made of pine branches covered with moss. His breath came in harsh gasps. In spite of the cold, he had tossed aside the thin blanket that had covered him.

"Grandfather." The boy knelt by the old man and spoke softly. "Wake up."

His paper-thin eyelids fluttered. Black eyes stared at them vacantly; then the lids closed again.

"Grandfather!"

"Oh, Eben," Penny whispered. "He's real sick."

"Malaria, maybe more," Eben said. "Let's get him to the fire."

The boy made no protest as Eben lifted the frail body and strode back through the clearing. Josh hurried to build up the fire as Penny pulled a bearskin from the wagon. Eben laid his burden on the skin and wrapped the folds around him.

"He's burning with the fever," he told Penny.

"I'll get some medicine."

The boy crept close to the motionless figure and crouched, watching silently. The dog did the same. Josh spoke from across the fire, keeping his distance from the bare fangs. "Are you from the Glades?" he asked. The boy shook his head without turning.

Josh tried again. "Then where are you from?"

This time the boy gave him a dark, measuring look. Still there was no answer. Eben signaled Josh over his head. "Later," he said quietly.

Josh got up and brought the other bearskin from the wagon. He hunched into it and sat watching his mother prepare the fever tea. His mouth puckered at the thought of the bitter tea, and he was glad that it wasn't for him. He went back to his inspection of the Indian. The boy looked to be about Josh's age. His thinness was lean, not bony like Josh's, and his features were sharp and angular. Occasionally, when he glanced up, the firelight reflected in his dark eyes almost as it reflected in the eyes of the wild animals Josh and Eben hunted at night. Then the thick brows would come together and the light would be replaced by impenetrable shadows.

The dog looked more like a wolf than a dog. Sensing Josh's attention, he turned his head and looked directly at Josh. Josh shivered. *I was worried about ghosts and snakes,* he thought. *And out of nowhere comes a boy called Tiger and a dog that looks like a wolf. Where did they come from? And why were they hiding?*

Chapter Four
Tiger in Yonder Hammock

When dawn came, the labored breathing of the old man had eased. Josh woke in the wagon and knew that his father had moved him after he had fallen asleep at the fire. He got up quickly, realizing that neither his father nor his mother would have left the fire.

He thought his feet made no sound in the damp sand, but Penny looked up as he approached. She placed her finger to her lips. Josh followed her gaze and saw the boy curled up next to his grandfather. "Let them rest," Penny whispered. "You can help your Pa water the animals while I start breakfast. He's already taken a bucket to Ornery."

Josh nodded and went back to the wagon for the other bucket. When he crossed the clearing again on his way to the spring, the wolf dog stood up and stretched. Josh took a strip of dried venison from his mother and held it out. When the dog lurched forward, Josh dropped the strip quickly. The dried meat disappeared in one gulp. The dog looked up inquiringly.

"Can he have another, Ma?" Josh asked. "He's real hungry."

"Wasting good food on that dog," Penny said disapprovingly, but she held out half of another piece. "He looks half-wild. I warrant he can catch his own meals."

"Probably." Josh watched the dog pace around the fire to lie back down beside the old man and his grandson. "But he won't leave until he thinks they're safe."

"It's possible. Dogs are like that."

"My dog will be," Josh said wistfully. "He'll be my own, and we'll take care of each other forever."

Penny turned back to the fire. "The Lord already gave you a horse. You'll get your dog when He is ready," she said. "Now off with you."

Josh left the clearing and followed the narrow, weedy path down through the knee-high bracken. He kicked at the fronds bent under the weight of the light frost and watched as they curled limply downward. Parting the fronds, he saw the tracks of a fox overlying that of a deer. Further along, both sets of tracks were joined with those of other animals. Though wary of the campfire, they had still come to drink at the Spaniard's spring, walking secretly through the night shadows.

When he reached the spring, Josh dropped the pail on the sloping bank and sought the beginning of the water. The water was clear and the sand boil was easy to locate. It bubbled out from under a large boulder of limestone, feeding the spring from its underground source. Josh picked up a fallen magnolia leaf and flipped it into the boil. It spun crazily around and around, then bobbed free, its glossy surface wet and shining.

Josh climbed out onto the rock, shivering as the icy water flowed over his bare feet. Then, from his vantage point, he surveyed the spring. Last night the creeping mist had been wisps of foglike gray. Now the rising sun colored it to match the inside of the conch shell Ma kept on the mantel at the cabin. The moss that covered the magnolias and cypress seemed to glow with an inner light. Even the ragged leaves of the strangler fig and wild scuppernong vine were edged with the pale fire. Josh forgot his errand and lost himself in the magic of sunrise.

A twig snapped above him and broke the spell. He glanced back up the trail. Willie Tiger slid down the last few feet and, avoiding a root that snaked up into the path, leaped down onto the bank. Silently, he picked up the pail Josh had dropped and filled it with water. Josh flushed. "I can do that."

Willie Tiger didn't answer. He turned and started back up the trail. Josh followed, his feeling of peace destroyed. Penny looked up as the two boys passed the fire. She started to say something, then changed her mind.

The ox had already been watered. The boys took the water to the horses. Josh ran his hand over Midnight's neck as the horse drank, blowing noisily. Then he made a curry comb from a dry palmetto leaf and scraped some of the dust out of the horse's coat. He talked softly as he worked, forgetting the Indian boy in his pleasure. The horse responded, nickering.

When he realized Willie Tiger was doing the same for the other horse, he watched from behind the shelter of Midnight's mane. The Indian boy's palmetto comb was a careful copy of Josh's. He was currying the other horse in the same manner that Josh had done, but his strokes were slow and wary. The horse shied uneasily away from the uncertain movements, and the boy dodged. Shaking its mane, the horse broke away and trotted across the corral.

Josh ducked his head and rubbed his horse's flank. When he looked up again, Willie Tiger had returned to the fire. Josh walked over to his father. "Did you see that, Pa?" he asked. "If these are Seminole horses, how come he's afraid of them?"

"He's probably never been around horses, Josh. Remember I told you that the Seminoles are not allowed to keep horses or cattle. I imagine there's a lot that Willie Tiger doesn't know."

"He sure doesn't act like it."

Eben adjusted the harness on the ox. "He's had a hard life, son. Don't expect him to warm up to strangers right away."

Later, as Ornery slowly pulled the wagon across the scrub, Josh tried without success to talk to the boy. Penny and Eben rode on the wagon seat, and Willie's grandfather lay in the back of the wagon. Willie Tiger and Josh sat cramped into the little space not filled up with supplies. Each conversation Josh started was cut off with a blunt yes or no from Willie Tiger. And when the wagon swayed, jolting Willie into Josh, the Indian boy held himself stiffly, pulling away as quickly as possible.

Josh sighed. *If I wait for him to warm up, I'll freeze to death,* he thought. He dug a store of pebbles from his pocket and scrabbled around in his belongings until he found his slingshot. For the rest of the trip, he amused himself by knocking dead fronds off palmettos. From time to time, he felt Willie's eyes on him. When he looked up, the boy was always looking at something else. The awkwardness destroyed Josh's enjoyment of the trip. He was glad when they reached Yonder Hammock, and the wagon stopped in the clearing.

For three days the man called Daniel Ogalla hung between life and death. Penny nursed him as best she could. Willie Tiger stayed in the barn loft, seldom moving from his grandfather's side, watching every move Penny made. On the fourth day the fever broke.

"He's going to be all right," Penny told the boy, not trying to hide the relief in her own voice. "He'll be all right."

Willie Tiger's face lightened, and some of the tension drained out of his thin body. "Thank you," he said soberly. "He would have died. I could do nothing."

Penny watched him stretch to relieve the stiffness of his tired muscles. "Go on outside," she said gently. "I'll come and get you when he asks for you."

The boy nodded, then climbed stiffly down the rough ladder to the barn floor. The dog rose from the dirt and whined. Willie Tiger knelt to rub behind the dog's ears. "He's better," he said quietly.

The crack of a whip shattered the quiet of the clearing. "Hiyah! Get in there!" The shouts mingled with the bawling of enraged cattle and the thunder of hooves. The racket drew Willie Tiger to the open barn door. For a moment he stood still, dog at his heels, blinking in the bright sunlight.

Josh and Eben fought their third cow into the holding pen. The cow slammed into the side of the pen, raking the rails with her jagged horns. Josh slid off Midnight and watched as the other cows spooked and raced around the pen, bawling in fear.

"Are you sure this is what you want, Pa?" he asked, wiping his face with his bandanna. "Seems like a difficult way to earn a living."

Eben leaned on the saddle horn. "I didn't say it'd be easy, son. But you and your ma deserve more than a dirt-poor scrub farm, and believe it or not, these cows will see that you get it. These old yellowhammers are our future. Just think of them as gold on the hoof—they'll look a lot better."

"Well, they sure don't look like good eating," Josh replied. "I'd rather chew on alligator tail than on them bony hides."

He turned and saw Willie Tiger. "Look, Pa."

Eben rode over to the boy. "Is your grandfather better?"

Willie Tiger nodded. "He sleeps now. The fever is gone."

"Good." Eben's gaze lingered on the lonely figure. "Want to give us a hand?"

The boy nodded. "You are chasing cattle?"

Eben grinned. "Well, I'd like to say catching cattle, but you're right. Mostly, we're chasing them. Come on, you can ride behind me."

He gave the boy a hand up, and they rode into the scrub. Josh followed, urging Midnight into a gallop. They passed the spotted horse in a blur of dust and disappeared around the bend. By the time Eben and Willie Tiger caught up, Josh had flushed a big bull out of a bay thicket. It trotted heavily into the open, bawling and rattling its horns.

"The problem is to get it back to the corral," Eben told Willie Tiger. "We've already tried roping, but neither one of us can hit a dead cow, much less a live one that won't stay still."

They watched as Josh and Midnight raced back and forth, always staying one step ahead of the bull. "That black horse is plumb gonna wear itself out trying," Eben said. "He's got pluck, I can say that for him."

Below them, the dog leapt forward, barking.

"Back, Moki." Willie Tiger's command held a touch of alarm. Moki slunk back at the horse's heels. Willie motioned toward an oak tree at the edge of the hammock. "If you can drive the cow under there, I could drop a rope around its neck."

"Maybe." Eben thought a minute, then agreed. "It might work."

When Willie Tiger was stationed on a low-hanging limb, Eben and Josh went to work. Eben rode on one side of the bull, cracking his whip. Josh rode on the other, waving his hat in the air. Together, they zigzagged back and forth through the brush until they finally drove the bull under the tree. On the first pass, Willie Tiger missed completely. On the second, the rope slid harmlessly off the bull's back. On the third, it looped neatly over the bull's horns.

With an enraged roar, the bull charged off. The limb Willie had wrapped the rope around cracked, and Willie

Tiger hit the ground. He bounced along in the sand, still holding the rope.

"Let go, Willie," Eben yelled. "Let go!"

Moki streaked across the sand toward the bull. He circled the animal, barking wildly. It stopped and lowered its horns, watching the dog.

Eben galloped past them and, leaning forward, held out his hand to Willie Tiger. The boy scrambled up behind Eben.

Just as the bull charged, Moki leaped forward. He fastened his teeth in the bull's nose and swung. Both bull and dog somersaulted through the air. When the bull got to his feet, the dog was already poised and waiting. The bull shook his head as if to clear it, then stood motionless, watching the dog.

"Did you see that, Pa? Did you see that dog?"

"A catch dog! That's a catch dog!" Eben hollered to Josh. "Why, he can bring those cows in almost without help. All we have to do is lead the way!"

"A catch dog?" Willie Tiger looked at Moki.

"Didn't you know?"

Willie Tiger looked at them solemnly. "If I had, I wouldn't have been up that tree."

Eben and Josh grinned; then they burst into laughter. Whooping and yelling, they went back to work. In no time, the bull was in the pen. By the time Daniel Ogalla was up and moving around, more than two dozen wild cattle filled the pen. They crowded about, trampling the ground and slamming against the rails until they creaked.

"Look, Grandfather," Willie told him. "Moki and I helped gather the wild cattle."

Eben squatted down beside the old man. "We've been using your dog, with your grandson's help. Without them, we'd still be popping the same stray out of the brush over and over again."

"I am glad they could in some way repay your kindness," the old man said with dignity. "We have little."

"Payment wasn't necessary." Eben's smile was warming. "We are glad the Lord spared your life."

"Your wife is a good nurse. The owl of death returned to her nest. She will wait for another day." Daniel pulled the blanket close in spite of the heat.

Eben noticed his movement. "Why don't we go inside? Penny has supper almost ready."

He helped the old man up and led him to the house. Josh and Willie Tiger followed, stopping at the bucket on the porch to clean up. After supper, Eben read from Exodus. Willie Tiger sat with his head bowed, and Josh couldn't see his eyes, but he noticed that Daniel listened carefully.

When Eben finished, Daniel said quietly, "We go home, too. Like your Moses. We left Florida with Billy Bowlegs when Willie was just a baby in my daughter's arms. She got sick on the journey and died on the boat. Willie's father, his grandmother, and I went on alone. For years we stayed in strange land. Many of our people died. Last year, sickness took Willie's grandmother. Then his father. Only Willie Tiger and I are left."

The old man paused and looked at the boy beside him. "When the owl calls my name, my grandson must not be left alone. He must be with his own family. I have another son who did not go with Billy Bowlegs. He is deep in what the white people call the Everglades. I take Willie Tiger to him."

"I see," Eben said slowly. "You have come a long way."

"Yes. Now I am afraid I can go no farther."

Penny looked at him sympathetically. "You could take them, couldn't you, Eben? When you take the cattle to Punta Rassa?"

"We are rounding up cattle," Eben told Daniel Ogalla. "When we have enough, we will drive them southwest to the ocean. There they will be loaded on boats and taken to Cuba. Your people are south of Punta Rassa. You and your grandson can go with us. It will ease your journey and be safer, too."

"You have been too kind," the old man protested. "We have no way of returning your kindness."

"Yes, you do," Eben said. He leaned forward, his face earnest in the lamplight. "We have no dog. With Moki and Willie, we could finish what we set out to do much faster. Without them we can't. We can help each other."

The old man reached out a bony hand. "Yes, Eben Bramlett. We will help each other."

The next few weeks Eben and Josh were up at dawn, popping cows out of the brush. Willie Tiger insisted on joining them, taking his turn in the saddle along with the other two. At first, Josh had been unwilling to let Willie ride Midnight, fearing the boy's lack of riding skill would endanger them both. But the Indian boy learned quickly and was soon galloping along easily. Josh noticed with some annoyance that the boy probably rode better than he did. When Eben praised the boy, Josh had to stifle the thought that having a Tiger at Yonder Hammock was not something he liked.

However, even he had to admit the work went faster with Willie Tiger there. Daniel Ogalla had said that the little Indian ponies were called *marshtackies*. The three workers spelled each other on the two untiring horses. Soon, the holding pen was filled.

Chapter Five
Arcadie

"Pa! Pa! That crazy old bull knocked down one of the rails!"

Eben grabbed his whip and ran for the holding pen. The cattle were milling about restlessly, stirred up by the splintering sounds as the bull threw himself against the rails. Eben's whip popped like a gunshot, but the bull just shook his head dumbly and continued his destruction.

"Here," Eben handed the whip to Josh. "Keep poppin' that stubborn mule. I'll try fixin' the rail."

He and Willie Tiger worked frantically to get another rail in place before the last one splintered. Moki raced back and forth along the side, barking at the bull. Daniel Ogalla left the porch and came to watch. "Why put the cattle in a pen?" he asked.

Eben stared at him. "How else could I claim them as mine?"

"If they stay there, they will sicken and die," the old man said. "They must run free to eat the marsh grass. Without its salt, they will not prosper. Put your brand on them and let them run free until the drive. Then you must make your home with them."

"You mean follow them?"

41

"Yes. They will fatten on good grass. You will follow in wagon. This is what my people do when we have cattle."

"That makes sense," Eben said slowly. "Instead of driving the cattle like we did during the war, we'll follow them. And instead of losing weight, they'll gain weight!"

He grabbed Penny around the waist and swung her around. "That's it, Penny! That's it!"

Flustered, Penny hit him on the shoulder. "Put me down, Eben Bramlett. Right this minute!"

Eben's exuberance disappeared. "Just think, Penny," he coaxed. "All that wonderful country—why, it'll be like a long camping trip."

"How long?" she asked.

"Well, April'll be here 'fore you know it. The grass is already greening. If we get the yellowhammers gathered, why, we could leave by May. We'd have from May to August to get them to Punta Rassa."

"Four months?"

"Ma, it's be a lot better'n being left behind," Josh pleaded. "Let's do it."

"Can I take my rocker?"

"Sure, Penny, sure. And everything'll be safe here. Most people never come out this far."

"Just you try to leave me behind," Penny said, her eyes dancing with laughter. "I was beside myself trying to figure out a way to get you to take me along!"

The next four weeks went by in a blur for Josh. Up at dawn, popping cows out of the brush, burning in a Rocking B, and releasing the cow to repeat the process again and again. By nightfall he was so tired that he fell into bed already half-asleep.

"One full-grown man and two yearlings won't be enough to drive cattle across the width of Floridy," Eben told Penny one night. "You'll be taking care of Daniel and cooking. We need another cowhand."

"Then why don't you go get one?" Penny smiled wryly, knowing Eben had already come to that conclusion. Eben grinned. "That's what I figured on doing. I'll be back in a few days. Josh and Willie Tiger'll take care of you."

"Eben," Penny stopped him, speaking seriously. "I want you to take Josh with you."

When Eben looked surprised, Penny explained. "Right now, he's having to share your attention with Willie Tiger. And he and Willie work all right together, but they don't really get along well. Not like two boys ought to, alone in the scrub. Willie Tiger doesn't trust Josh yet. Josh understands, but things around here have changed too fast for him. And not in the way he really wanted. Remember, he has always been your partner—not just another hand."

"I see," Eben said. "I guess I have been pretty busy lately. It'll give us time to catch up."

The days on the trail to Kissimmee were special to Josh. "Ya-hoo," he yelled, cantering Midnight around in the road. "I've got the spring jim-jams, Pa!"

Eben laughed, feeling the same. Green covered the scrub, erasing the brown of winter. Bees hummed in the palmetto blossoms and buzzed in the magnolias. "It's a new time, son. A new time for us, too."

They rode into Kissimmee well before noon the second day. Eben found them a room at the only hotel and went in search of a ranch hand. He returned an hour later, his errand uncompleted, but his enthusiasm high. "Cattle business is booming, partner," he told Josh. "The dealers are offering from eight to thirteen dollars a head down in Punta Rassa. In gold, Cuban gold! And we must have branded near a thousand of them steers. If we fatten 'em up on the drive, we ought to get thirteen a head easy."

"That's great," Josh replied, a little absently. "Pa, did you find a drover?"

"No luck atall, son. Not many drifters in town," Eben said. "Most have jobs, and the ones that don't aren't interested in anything but whiskey."

"Or food." Josh grinned. "Let's go eat. I want you to meet someone."

Outside the restaurant, a man lounged on a bench. His shirt and pants might once have been different colors. Now they were the same shade of dingy gray. His boots, covered with dust and fitted over long, narrow feet, were old and cracked. Dirt obscured his nationality and hid the original color of his hair and beard. He looked to weigh no more than a hundred and ten pounds and that stretched out to a six-foot length. His eyes were closed.

"I thought I had seen long and lean before," Eben said in awe, "but that's the hungriest-looking feller I've ever laid eyes on. Is he dead?"

"Not yet. His name's Arcadie," Josh said. "And he hasn't eaten in four days. I told him to wait here for us."

"Well, son. I don't know if we got enough to rescue every stray off the street." At Josh's dismayed look, Eben ran his fingers over the few coins in his pocket. "But I guess we have enough for this one," he added doubtfully. "Hope he doesn't eat as much as he looks like he needs to eat."

When Josh touched his shoulder, the man sat up and pushed back his slouch hat. His cavernous eyes burned bright blue out of the dark face, and a smile twitched the ragged mustache into a grotesque shape. "Howdy," he said, holding out his hand. "I'm Arcadie, and I hear you're lookin' for a hand."

Eben nodded, shaking the long, bony fingers. "Could be. Join us for a bite to eat?"

The smile became a twisted grin that lifted one side of his face a little higher than the other. Eben blinked.

"Thanks. You've got a mighty fine boy here," he said, patting Josh on the back. "Mighty fine."

"I know," Eben replied as he led the way to the table. "You have children?"

"Nope. Never married." Arcadie leaned back so that the waitress could pour his coffee. "Just leave the pot," he said.

Eben and Josh watched in amazement as Arcadie began to eat. He used his knife and fork neatly, but the food disappeared at an alarming rate.

"Were does he put it?" Josh asked after Arcadie motioned for his third refill.

Eben shrugged. He noticed that many of the diners had a bottle of liquor on the table. "Hope you don't drink," he asked.

Arcadie didn't bother to smother his burp. "Never touch the stuff. Weak stomach."

"Where you from?"

"Down Arcadie way. That's where I got my name." Arcadie handed Josh one of the remaining biscuits and a pot of homemade jam. "Have some jam."

"What's your real name?"

"I forgot."

Eben's eyebrows raised. "How old are you?"

Arcadie did some quick mental calculations. "Uh, twenty-eight—no, must be thirty-two."

"Done any cattle work?"

Arcadie's mustache quivered. "A little."

"I'm looking for a man to help me drive cattle to Punta Rassa. It'll take about four months."

"How much are you paying?"

Josh gave his father an uneasy look.

Eben replied evenly. "Pay comes at the end of the trail."

"Well, thanks for the meal," Arcadie said, uncoiling his length from the chair. "Hope you find your man." He scooped the last biscuit from the table.

"My ma's the best cook in Floridy," Josh said craftily. "She can cook better'n this any day of the week."

Arcadie stopped.

"Her biscuits are so light they'd float iff'n they weren't held down, and she can make gator meat taste like beef," Josh elaborated. "And huckleberry pie—why, nobody's is juicier."

"Is the boy telling the truth?" Arcadie turned to Eben.

"He's stretching a mite," Eben acknowledged, "but not much."

"When'll you be ready to pull out?" Arcadie asked.

"First thing in the morning," Eben replied.

"You got your man," he said, holding out his hand. Eben shook it firmly. "I'll get my gear and meet you here at dawn."

When he left, Josh turned to his father. "He'll be great, Pa. You'll see. You should have heard the tales he told me this morning."

"I can imagine," Eben said dryly. "I've heard that Arcadia men are a rough bunch. But he doesn't drink, and he'll hire on for food. Maybe he'll be like the marsh-tackies and be one of the Lord's blessings in disguise." He surveyed the remains of the meal in amazement. "I sure hope we can afford to feed him."

Later that night, they got a demonstration of Arcadie's talents. It was payday on the ranches, and the cowboys roared into town for a little celebrating. Three of them had stayed too long in the saloon and had turned ugly. When Eben and Josh passed them on the street, they followed, calling them "backwoods crackers" and a lot of other names Josh didn't recognize. Just as Eben turned to face them, Arcadie appeared out of the night. His shadow stretched arrow-straight across the walk.

"Move on," he told the men, his deep-set eyes steely in the light from the saloon window.

"Who says?" they retorted, reaching for their guns.

Before they could clear leather, they were looking down the barrel of a Colt .44. Josh hadn't even seen the movement required to draw it. Neither had the men. They backed away and decided to have another drink.

Arcadie tipped his tattered hat to Eben and Josh. "See you in the morning, boss. That is, if you're through sightseeing."

Eben nodded wordlessly, and Arcadie slouched back into the night. "Whew, Josh. I think we've found us another marshtackie."

Josh's eyes gleamed with excitement. "Did ya see that, Pa? Did ya? Arcadie's gun came out of that holster like lightning!"

He followed his father down the street, pulling an imaginary gun out of an imaginary holster and shooting at lighted windows. "Blam, blam! I bet he's a gunslinger, Pa."

"I hope not," Eben said, frowning at Josh's enthusiasm. "You know how your ma feels about weapons. We need a cowhand, not a gunslinger."

"Ma'll like him, won't she, Pa?"

Eben grinned, suddenly in a good humor. "Maybe after he's been in her wash pot a couple of hours. Wonder what he'll look like when she gets through with him?"

Chapter Six
Cracking Whips

Arcadie stood in the doorway of the cabin, hat in hand. His skin, though dry and leathery, was as clean as a newborn calf's, and his clothes had been scrubbed to a soft gray.

"If I'd a know'd a bath was part of the job, ma'am, I believe I'd a stayed in town," he drawled, rubbing the whiskers that had turned out to be dark blonde. After a good scrubbing with Ma's homemade herbal soap, his hair ringed his thin face in a soft halo. No amount of stroking could get the locks to smooth back down.

Josh smothered a grin. Arcadie had lost his dangerous look and resembled nothing more than a cattail just bursting open. "You look fine, Arcadie," he said solemnly. "You should see the rest of us when Ma has a bath day."

Penny sniffed. "A little hot water and soap never hurt anybody. Now on with you. Supper'll be a little late tonight."

Arcadie clumped away, muttering under his breath. "Baths and a bunch of Injuns. Injuns!"

Josh frowned. Neither he nor his father had stopped to consider what Arcadie's reaction to the Seminoles would be. In the next few days, it became apparent that the feelings ran high on both sides. Arcadie refused to sleep in the loft with Daniel Ogalla and Willie Tiger. He took a bedroll to the porch every night and slept with his gun belt near and his rifle by his side. He spoke to Willie Tiger only when it was necessary in the line of work. Other than that, he ignored his presence.

Willie Tiger responded with sullenness. Had his grandfather been able to travel, Josh knew Willie would have drifted away in the night. Only the courtesy of Josh's parents and the dignity of Daniel Ogalla kept a smooth surface on the troubled waters.

Josh watched Arcadie thoughtfully, wondering why he stayed. He moved across to the corral, remembering the surprise both he and his father had felt when Arcadie turned up with two well-fed, healthy cow ponies. Now his father rode one of them, and Willie Tiger rode the other marshtackie. And for the first time, Josh wondered where Arcadie had got the horses. Then, feeling guilty for his suspicions, he climbed through the rails and joined Arcadie.

"Better git that hat on, boy. It's gonna be hot enough to fry skeeters on the wing," Arcadie said. He jammed his own slouch hat onto his head and swung easily into the saddle. "Your pa's sending you and me to Crane's Hammock this morning. He saw about a dozen cows over there yestiday."

"Where is Pa?"

"He and that Injun boy went down near the crick with the big herd. They left early."

Josh sighed. Arcadie's problem with Willie Tiger meant that Josh never got to ride with his father anymore. The resentment that swept over him was no longer a surprise. Sometimes he felt like an overgrown turkey buzzard being shoved out of the nest. He mounted Midnight and whirled him around to charge through the gate after Arcadie.

For a while they let the horses run. When the tenseness disappeared from both the boy and horse, Josh settled into an easy trot. Arcadie had already stopped his big bay. Josh watched as the startlingly blue eyes scanned the scrub. Then Arcadie turned in the saddle to look south. Days of hot, dusty work had settled his hair down, and again he had a lean look.

"See something?" Josh asked.

"Maybe, maybe not," was the noncommittal answer. Arcadie favored Josh with one of his grotesque grins, to soften his words, and changed the subject. "You've growed, boy. I think you've shot up a foot since I've been here."

Josh grinned back. "It's Ma's cooking."

Arcadie nodded. "She's a good cook, just like you said. You tole the truth about that. Always tell the truth, boy. A man's word is his bond."

"Yes, sir."

"Before we get to the hammock, we'll stop for a little target practice again," Arcadie promised. "Okay?"

"You bet!"

Later, Arcadie set rocks on a fallen log and handed Josh the Colt. A few weeks of practice had paid off. Each time Josh squeezed the trigger, a puff of dust appeared where a rock had been. Arcadie rubbed his thick mustache. "You're a natural, Josh. Wouldn't be surprised if you beat me someday."

Josh spun the empty gun, pretending to draw from the hip. "When are you going to teach me to clear leather?"

"Don't be in such a hurry." Arcadie refilled the chamber and put the gun back into his holster. "Shootin's one thing, clearing leather's another."

They made short work of gathering the cattle. Eben had bought three more rawhide whips in Kissimmee, one for each rider. Eighteen-feet long, the lash snapped out in a crack almost as satisfying to Josh as the pistol shots. A rider on either side of a herd could really get the cows moving. By noontime, Josh and Arcadie drove their cows into the big herd that was grazing on the river grass.

Eben broke away and galloped up to them. His horse left a trail of dust in the heat. "I heard shooting," he said, a questioning look in his gray eyes.

"I gave the boy some more target practice," Arcadie said. "He's coming along real good."

Eben frowned, looking at Josh. "It don't hurt to learn to shoot good," he warned. "Just don't get carried away with it."

"Okay, Pa." Josh stood up in the stirrups to look at the herd. Willie Tiger rode along the fringes, keeping the cows bunched up. Occasionally one would bolt out of the herd, only to be quickly rounded up by Moki. "We got enough, now?"

"We got enough," Eben replied. "It's time to move out."

Excitement surged through Josh. "When, Pa? When?"

"In the morning." Eben leaned over to ruffle Josh's hair. "Your ma's been packing all day. Reckon we'll be ready."

That night, everyone helped with preparations to leave. Four months on the move meant supplies and equipment had to be chosen carefully and packed tightly. Arcadie had drawn diagrams of supply wagons used on long drives. He and Eben put a canvas top over the wagon, providing protection from the elements. Ma filled compartments with cooking supplies, pots and pans, bedrolls, canvas, and anything else she thought might be needed. When she finished, she brought out her rocker to be lashed on back. Arcadie raised his eyebrows, but said nothing to endanger his enjoyment at mealtimes.

Josh thought sure he would be the first up the next morning. He slipped outside in the predawn, closing the door carefully to avoid waking his parents. A full moon hung in the sky, bathing the clearing in light and shadow. Josh leaned against a porch post and watched, listening to the soughing of the wind in the pines and the quiet movements of the horses in the corral. When a shadow by the rails moved, Josh took a short breath and moved forward, ready to shout a warning.

"Relax."

Josh whirled around. Arcadie turned over in his blanket. "It's the old Indian. He's been out there for an hour or so."

"Daniel? What's he doing?"

"Probably some sort of ceremony." Arcadie's voice sounded bored, but Josh suspected he knew every move the old man had made. When Daniel moved slowly toward the barn, Josh stayed still, respecting his privacy. He sat down beside Arcadie.

"Maybe he's worried about Willie Tiger and Moki 'cause they stayed with the herd at the river. Or maybe he's saying good-bye to the place."

"Maybe. Full moon does strange things to folks."

Josh grinned. "What things?"

"Makes it hard to sleep, for one thing," Arcadie grumbled. "Gives folks the wanderin's when they should be in bed."

"How can you sleep? Today's the drive!"

"Easy." Arcadie rolled over and put his hat over his eyes. "Wake me for breakfast."

Josh sighed. He wandered out by the corral, trying to ease the waiting. Midnight nickered and thrust his nose over Josh's shoulder. He was sitting on the top rail when Penny lit the lamp in the cabin. She opened the door and lamplight spilled in a warm rectangle across the cool gray of the porch.

"Josh?"

"Out here, Ma."

She wrapped a shawl around her shoulders and joined him. "I thought I heard voices a while ago."

"I was talking to Arcadie. I couldn't sleep."

"Neither could I." The moon picked out silver lights in her unbound hair and softened the curves of her face.

"It's hard to imagine, driving cattle across most of Floridy. Your pa's a marvel, Josh. Don't you ever forget it."

"I won't, Ma."

Penny took a deep breath. "Then how about gettin' water for breakfast. We're going to need a huge pot of coffee to keep us going today. And a good, hearty breakfast."

"Pancakes?" Josh's voice was hopeful.

"Pancakes and eggs. Might as well use them up. Eggs don't travel."

"Yes, ma'am!"

Breakfast was finished before dawn. Penny took one last look at the cabin by lamplight, then locked the door. Daniel was settled in the wagon, and the horses were saddled, ready to go. Ornery led them out of the hammock, creaking slowly along.

Out in the scrub, Eben sent Josh and Arcadie ahead to spell Willie Tiger and to get the herd moving. Eben rode beside Penny until he was sure she could handle the wagon. When they reached the herd, it was already bunched and moving. Penny stopped the wagon to stare at the mass of bawling cattle. "Do you think we'll make it, Eben?" she whispered.

He took her hand. "We'll make it, Pen. I promise. And strange though our crew is, the Lord'll hold it together. You keep praying, Pen, and we'll make it all right."

By the time the sun rose, they were on their way south. Even Willie Tiger was affected by the moving stream of cattle. He rode back and forth, popping his whip as readily as Josh. "Move 'em out," Arcadie called, grinning at the boys. "Move 'em out!"

Chapter Seven
Shadows in the Night

The herd followed the river south, grazing on mineral-rich marsh grass. Any visions Josh had of flying over the prairie, cracking his whip, vanished under the paralyzingly slow pace. Even Ornery had no trouble keeping up with the grazing cattle.

"Won't they go any faster, Pa?" Josh complained. "Midnight's about to lie down and go to sleep."

"I hope not, Josh. This is more a grazing drive than a cattle drive," Eben replied. "We want them to eat and put some fat on their poor old bones. There's no hurry."

Dissatisfied, Josh rode back to the wagon. In three days, they had moved only two miles. Eben had unhitched the wagon and pitched the tent beside it. A rope corral held Ornery and the horses when they weren't needed. Penny had set up camp, humming to herself as she worked.

"What's the matter, Josh?" she asked when he dismounted.

"There's nothing to do." He sat down beside Daniel Ogalla, who was working with strips of hide and two long poles. He watched the old man's hands weave the strips in and out. Finally his natural curiosity took over and he asked, "What's that?"

The old man's smile crinkled the flesh around his eyes. "A travois for the water barrels. So they can be carried some distance to bring back water."

"But the river's right over there," Josh said.

"It will not always be so. Though the river will be close by, the thickets may prevent us from getting water in some places," Daniel replied calmly. He continued to lace strips of hide around the two poles. "And it gives me something to do."

"'Tis no good to be idle," his mother agreed. "If your pa doesn't need you and Willie Tiger, why don't you go fishing?"

Josh glanced at Daniel. The old man nodded. "It would be good," he said, holding Josh's gaze with his own. "Fish is good."

Sighing, Josh got up and pulled two bamboo poles out from under the wagon. The afternoon sun shimmered on the flat sea of grass and made a blinding mirror of the broad river curving through it. Josh found Willie Tiger on the far side of the herd, with Moki at his heels.

"Ma wants us to get some fish for supper," he said, gesturing toward the river with the poles.

Willie Tiger didn't answer but turned the marshtackie toward the water, commanding Moki to stay. When Josh caught up again, the horse was grazing near the water, unsaddled and hobbled. Willie Tiger had waded on out into the marshy reeds, water up to his knees.

Josh left the poles on the grass and splashed past him. When he reached deep water, he plunged in, swimming clumsily. Willie Tiger approached slowly and cautiously.

Josh slung wet hair out of his eyes and watched. "Can't you swim?"

"Yes." The boy recognized the challenge in Josh's voice and withdrew from it. Moving away, he slid silently into the water.

Josh dog-paddled, chagrined at the way that Willie Tiger's body cut smoothly through the water. "Where did you learn to swim like that?"

"On the reservation there was a river." Willie Tiger's quiet voice carried clearly across the water. "All the children swam. I learned from them."

His desire to learn new things kept Josh in the water, watching. When he tried to copy Willie Tiger's movements, he only splashed more water. Willie Tiger saw him and, without comment, swam closer so that Josh could see the strokes more clearly. By the time Willie was ready to get out, Josh was swimming a few yards, although without the grace of the older boy.

Afterward, the boys went upriver where the water was unmuddied. Dried scraps of biscuit on the hooks snared ten bream before the boys were willing to stop.

They took the fish to Penny, who fried them over the campfire. The scent brought Arcadie to the tent, taking deep breaths and groaning. "I hope you caught enough," he warned. "Fresh fish don't go far after the bones are picked."

"Still bored?" Penny asked as she slipped another fish onto Josh's plate.

Surprised in spite of himself, Josh shook his head. The afternoon that had threatened to drag on forever had disappeared into a memory. He ate the last fish more slowly, savoring the smoked flavor of the white meat. When he finished, he lay back sleepily.

"Don't get too relaxed," Eben teased. "You and Willie Tiger have the first watch."

"Um."

"You can rest a while. Then both of you can ride herd a couple of hours," Eben told them. "Then Arcadie will take a turn, then me."

A light breeze came off the river at dusk, rippling the grass. Josh and Willie Tiger folded their whips and mounted. Willie Tiger hesitated, then gave a sharp command to Moki. The dog trotted over to stand at Midnight's heels. "You take Moki tonight," Willie Tiger said. "Tomorrow he will go with me."

Josh could only nod, speechlessly, as Willie Tiger galloped away. The dog followed Josh as readily as he had followed Willie Tiger, trotting toward the river side of the herd. They began a slow circle. At first, Josh had no trouble staying awake. The moonlight had paled to gray and clouds sometimes obscured the moon, but he could see some distance away. Finally the sameness of the night landscape lulled him and he began to drift, letting Midnight pick his own way around the herd. About an hour later, a low rumble from Moki woke him. He glanced around quickly and saw nothing. "You probably saw Willie Tiger," he told the dog. "Though I'm surprised you'd growl at him. I thought dogs could see at night."

Moki stiffened and growled again. He stood facing the scrub in the distance. Josh stared into the night, but could only see the line of dark where the scrub began, nothing else. Moki's stance made the back of his neck prickle. He looked out over the herd of cattle. They seemed quiet and contented. Josh began to sing quietly, to calm both Moki and himself.

When Arcadie rode out to relieve him, he described Moki's behavior. Arcadie tensed and stared toward the scrub as Josh had done. Nothing moved in the night. "Probably nothing," he told Josh. "Willie's already at the tent. Make sure you shake out the bedding before you curl up."

"Sure."

Josh was almost asleep before he reached the tent. He barely remembered Arcadie's warning but managed to shake out the blanket before he curled up next to his father. The next thing he knew, the sun was streaming through the open side of the tent.

Willie Tiger was rolling up his bedroll, and Josh hastened to do the same. Arcadie and Eben were gone. So was Moki. Penny saw them and called, "Come and eat, sleepyheads! We're packing up today."

"Why?" Josh said, scrubbing the sleep out of his face with his hands. When he stepped outside the tent, he found they were alone in the grass sea. Not a cow was in sight. "What happened?"

"Your pa and Arcadie moved the cattle downriver. Look," she replied, pointing to the south. "There."

Josh could just make out a line of dark where yesterday the grass had met the sky in an unbroken line. "That's them?"

"Um-hm. Now eat up and you can help me break camp."

Breakfast disappeared in a hurry. Josh could never understand why food tasted better when eaten outdoors, but he knew that it did. Evidently Willie Tiger agreed. His plate was scraped clean.

Willie Tiger put the bedrolls in the wagon and folded the tent while Josh harnessed Ornery. Then they dismantled and rolled up the rope corral. Penny climbed onto the seat. Josh and Willie Tiger helped Daniel up beside her. As Josh held the old man's arm, he was shocked at its birdlike thinness. His glance met his mother's, and she shook her head gently.

The horses were already saddled. When Josh and Willie Tiger mounted, they could barely hold them in. Penny laughed and waved them on ahead. Yelling, they raced across the grass toward the moving herd. Josh reached them first, but only a few yards in front of Willie Tiger. Josh acknowledged the older boy's improvement in riding with a wave of his hat, then galloped toward his father.

"Pa!"

Eben wheeled the roan and waited. Josh stopped alongside him. "Where are we going?"

"South," Eben replied. "Arcadie said Moki was restless last night. We figured to move out away from the scrub and stay away from the woods whenever we can."

"Why, Pa?"

"When I drove for Jacob Summerlin up on the Alachua prairies, wolves circled the herd and the cows stampeded. I almost got run over that night. I don't know what Moki heard. We never saw anything, and that's what bothers me. We'll keep the herd moving today. Maybe we'll leave trouble behind."

Josh shivered, thinking about the warning Moki had given. What would he have done if wolves had attacked the herd?

Each night, he and Willie Tiger rode first watch. Moki no longer stayed with either boy, but restlessly circled the herd on his own. Sleep no longer threatened Josh on the watch. He rode tensely, expecting each moment for wolves to spring out of the grass.

The second week, they were forced to funnel the herd down a narrow strip of land where a stretch of slash pine curved toward the river.

"Tonight," Daniel Ogalla said, pointing to the dark ribbon of pines. "They will come tonight."

"We'll hold the herd and wait until morning to drive them down by the woods," Eben said. "We'll circle them here and ride watch all night."

They bunched the herd together and let Moki keep the stragglers in. Each rider carried his whip. Arcadie took his rifle and Eben his shotgun. "How about letting Josh take my handgun?" Arcadie asked. "He can shoot."

Eben hesitated. "All right." He gave Josh a long, steady look. "Think before you fire, son. And be careful. If the wolves don't spook the cattle, the gunfire will. Keep 'em moving in a circle."

Josh nodded and strapped on the gun belt, a little shakily. They rode two to each side of the herd, carrying flambeaus. They moved constantly, working to keep the cattle bunched. The herd was restless. When the first howl came out of the dark, they began to bawl and mill about frantically.

"Keep 'em turning on themselves," Arcadie shouted, racing past Josh, popping his whip. For the next few minutes, Josh had no time to think of the howls. He and Midnight leaped back and forth, cracking the whip, trying to keep the cattle from stampeding into a full run. He heard a rifle shot, deeper and fuller than the popping of the whips, but he could see nothing. Up and down he rode, working the cows back in.

At first he thought the creeping form in the grass was Moki. Then the light from the flambeau glittered on bared fangs. Josh urged Midnight forward, thrusting the flame at the wolf. It slunk back, only to be joined by two others. Quickly Josh wrapped the whip around the saddle horn and drew his gun. Forcing himself to think of rocks, he fired three shots. Two wolves fell and the other disappeared into the grass.

Josh wheeled back to the herd. In spite of all he could do, cows broke away from the main body and ran headlong into the dark. He heard the roar of his father's shotgun, then another shot from the rifle. Then the wolves were gone.

The rest of the night was spent in settling the herd. The whips were folded, for now any movement might set them off. The riders circled slowly, singing to calm the cattle. When morning came, Josh was swaying in the saddle from fatigue.

The early light was gray and merciless as it picked out the still forms of dead wolves and a few fallen cows. Josh rode slowly back to the camp. Daniel sat near the fire, hunched into a blanket. Penny ran to meet Josh. "Is everyone all right?"

He nodded. "They're coming in."

Willie Tiger was last. "Where's Moki?" he asked without dismounting. Josh shook his head and looked at his father and Arcadie. Arcadie shrugged.

"I thought he was with you," Eben said.

Willie Tiger wheeled his horse around and started back to the herd. The others remounted and rode out. They found the dog in a bloodstained patch of grass near the river. A dead wolf lay beside him, its throat ripped out.

"He's hurt," Josh said, leaping down to look over Willie Tiger's shoulder. Willie Tiger didn't reply. He lifted the dog gently and put him across the saddle. They remounted and rode slowly back to camp.

Carefully he placed Moki at his grandfather's feet. Daniel Ogalla touched him gently with clawlike hands, probing for wounds. Willie Tiger waited.

"He will live," Daniel said finally. "He will get well."

The tenseness left Willie Tiger's shoulders, and he knelt beside the dog. Josh breathed sharply, suddenly realizing that he had been holding his breath.

Chapter Eight
Milk and Honey

The next few weeks went by without incident. June came and went in the golden haze of early summer. The cattle grew sleek and fat on the thick grass along the river. The steers lost in the attack of the wolves had provided steak for as long as the meat could be preserved. And there was no lack of wild meat for Penny to cook. The men found the wilderness bountiful in deer, turkey, quail, and other small animals. If all else failed, the river yielded fresh fish. When the flour ran low, Daniel showed Penny how to make koontie flour from the root of the sago palm, and never was a meal served without fresh biscuits. Even the angular bones of the boys disappeared under the abundance of food and the slow pace of life. Only Arcadie's frame still showed its skeleton, for though he ate more than the others, he remained as hungry-looking as ever.

It was sheer abundance that drove Arcadie to his folly. His forever-active appetite nearly satiated by food, he looked for that special something to round off the meals. Blackberries had ripened along the fringes of the woods. Big bowls of the blue-black berries set Arcadie to wishing for honey and cream to go along with the fruit. The cream wasn't too hard to find. One of the young cows had recently lost a calf, and her lowing advertised to all that she still carried milk.

Penny laughed when Arcadie told her what he wanted to do. "Milk a wild cow? You're liable to end up under her hooves."

"What if we tame her, Ma?" Josh rather liked the idea of milk and cream himself.

"If you can tame that young heifer, I'll milk her," Penny promised.

"Now's as good a time as any. I got a sure-fire way to tame that cow," Arcadie said. "Besides, she's just begging to be milked. Why, she'll thank us for doing her a favor." He jackknifed to a sitting position and reached for his rope. "Let's go, Josh."

Most of the cattle were down in the grass, seeking relief from the heat of the day. Everyone gathered to watch the fun. Arcadie and Josh approached the young cow cautiously from the rear. She turned her head to watch them, jaws moving back and forth on her cud. The horses cut her out of the herd easily, and Moki kept her separated until Arcadie could settle his rope around her head.

They drove her back to camp where she stood trembling under the rope. Arcadie threw one leg over the saddle horn and looked at the grinning spectators. He gave a nonchalant shrug, mustache raised at one corner in amusement.

"See, Ma," Josh called. "She's half-tamed already!"

When Arcadie and Josh dismounted and approached the frightened cow, she went into action. Fishtailing and bucking like an unbroken horse, she charged the rope. It was the first time Josh had seen Arcadie taken aback. The rope went slack and snapped around Arcadie's leg like a bear trap. The cow charged past, and the rope went taut before Josh could reach Arcadie. Yelling at the top of his lungs, the hapless cowboy bounced along after the cow. The spectators yelled happily back, shouting instructions to Arcadie.

On the second swoop past the tent, the enraged cow hit one of the tent poles. The tent folded and enveloped both the cow and Arcadie. The two of them tore across the thick grass, humping along like a gigantic caterpillar. They made one blind circle, then headed back toward the herd.

"Mount up, boys," Eben called. "If they spook that herd, we'll be working from now to next Sunday rounding them up."

It took all three riders and the dog to turn the frantic cow toward the river. She splashed into the shallows, where the water forced her to stop and stand shuddering under the canvas. They left her and dismounted to help Arcadie.

He was lying in a foot of water. "Are you all right, Arcadie?" Josh asked anxiously.

"'Course I am." Arcadie sat up, spitting water and shaking minnows out of his shirt. He fixed them with a steady glare, daring them to laugh. "I tamed 'er, didn't I?"

Eben and the boys watched in open-mouthed amazement as he got up and flipped the canvas off the cow. She walled her eyes but followed docilely as he led her back to camp, sloshing water from his boots at every step.

No one ever got Arcadie to admit he hadn't planned every step of the incident. The cow was hitched to the back of the wagon and provided enough milk for everyone until she went dry.

The honey was a different matter. Even Penny agreed that honey would be a good thing to have. Daniel sighted a beeline toward the woods. Arcadie, riding high after his success with taming the cow, suggested the boys go along to help bring back the honeycomb. Penny and Eben rigged up a protective covering of mosquito netting for each, and they set out to locate the honey tree.

They rode around the herd and entered the forest of slash pine. The underbrush was sparse, and the ground was covered with a thick carpet of pine needles that muffled the horses' hooves. Splashes of bright sunlight clashed with the deep purple shadows cast by the trees. Josh felt as if he were charging through a huge swarm of bright, transparent butterflies. When his eyes adjusted to the patterns of light and shadow, he could see that they were traveling along a slight ridge of ground. Here the pines grew tall and far apart. Farther down, in a slight ravine, myrtle and palmetto scrub grew thickly, blocking his view.

He turned back to see that the other two had ridden on ahead. He yelled and galloped after them. When he caught up, he yelled again, enjoying the sound of his voice in the vacuum of the forest. Arcadie grinned and hallooed back, and even Willie Tiger stood up in the stirrups and howled like a wolf. The sound wiped the grin from Arcadie's face, and he rode on ahead. The two boys followed, silent again.

Josh watched Willie Tiger as he rode. Though dressed in a pair of Josh's britches and one of Eben's old shirts, he would never have been mistaken for either of them. His body moved with the horse, as if the two were one. If he had not known better, Josh would have thought that the Indian boy had practically been born in the saddle. Shafts of sunlight flickered across his face as he rode, emphasizing the high cheekbones and shadowing his eyes. He held his head oddly. Josh wondered why, then suddenly realized that Willie Tiger was listening to the forest.

Surprised, he started to listen too. It took an effort to shut out the dull clopping of the hooves on the needles, the creaking of the saddles, and the jingling of the hardware on the harnesses. Finally, Josh heard the faint whir of wings and the rapid pattering made by the tiniest forest creatures scampering for safety. Then he heard the sound that had attracted Willie Tiger's attention.

At first Josh thought the cracking twig might have been a deer or another large animal. Then he heard another twig snap. Common sense told him that deer would never follow, only run. He glanced uneasily back but saw nothing in the shadows. His knees tightened around Midnight, urging her to close the distance between him and Willie Tiger.

He caught up, but when he opened his mouth to mention the noise, Willie Tiger's face looked so closed and forbidding that he didn't speak. Suddenly he realized that the months on the trail had relaxed the Indian boy. Though still quiet and withdrawn, he had gradually lost his original sullen suspicion. Now it was back.

They left the ridge and headed down into the ravine, picking their way through the myrtle. The big trees thinned out, to be replaced with magnolia, swamp maple, and a few big cypress. Heat hung heavily on the air as the ground grew damper. Finally, the horses plowed through the bottom muck and climbed back up the other side of the ravine.

Josh was glad to be back out into the pines. Something about the thicket had made him uneasy. He shook off the feeling as he caught a glimpse of Arcadie, just ahead. He caught up easily.

"I figure it ought to be right about there," Arcadie said, sighting toward the west. "You two keep up now."

Josh gave him a puzzled look, then realized Willie Tiger wasn't with them. The uneasy feeling returned. "Willie Tiger was between you and me. Didn't you see him?"

Arcadie made an impatient sound. "You know I don't keep up with that Injun."

Exasperated, he turned his horse and started back down into the thicket. "Probably hiding," he said unfairly, "wasting my time."

Josh followed, keeping close to Arcadie. They called and were answered by a nicker from the spotted horse. Willie Tiger was near the bottom of the ravine, lying face down in the muck. Josh slid off Midnight and ran to the boy. Arcadie remained on his horse, waiting.

Josh turned Willie Tiger over. A red crease ran across the side of his forehead and into his hair. A thin line of blood trickled down one temple. Willie Tiger opened his eyes and stared up fearfully. When he saw Josh, he struggled to sit up. Josh stepped back.

"What happened?" he asked.

"I-I—" he fingered the injury and made a disgruntled face. "I was not watching. I had my head turned. The horse jumped." He glanced at Arcadie's scornful expression. "I must have got hit by a branch," he admitted sullenly.

Arcadie gave a disgusted snort. "Thought as much. Let's go."

Josh waited until Willie Tiger mounted, then let him go ahead. He wasn't satisfied with Willie Tiger's explanation, but there was nothing he could do about it.

About fifteen minutes later, they found the bee tree. It was near a swamp, and a few inches of brackish water barred the way to it. They dismounted and tied the horses. Covering themselves with the netting, they splashed across to the tree. Arcadie lit a lighter knot and tore off part of his shirt. He started the rag burning, then thrust it into the bottom opening of the bee tree. "Get ready, boys," he said jubilantly. "Them bees'll come boiling out of the top."

They didn't have long to wait. An angry humming stirred in the tree as smoke began to drift out of the top.

"Here they come!"

Bees swarmed out of the top of the dead tree, and Josh felt like every one headed for him. He stumbled backward and began to run. Vaguely, he heard Arcadie yelling at him but the sound of buzzing echoed in his ears and he couldn't stop. Leaves slapped at him and branches clawed at the netting as he thrust his way through the

brush. Finally he could run no more and fell to the ground, the buzzing still all around him. Nothing happened. He stood up and shook his head, sending the folds of mosquito netting swaying outward. Two bees tumbled down from one of the folds, then buzzed angrily away, bright dots in the shadowed thicket.

Josh laughed weakly. "Arcadie," he called. There was no answer. A feather of fear rippled along Josh's neck. He looked around. There was nothing that he recognized. No landmark, no trail. He sat down suddenly. His years in the scrub had taught him enough to know that he was in danger. His foolishness had sent him plunging into the wilderness with no landmarks, no horse, no friends.

Fighting his fear, he prayed almost feverishly, waiting for calmness to return. After a while his pulse stopped racing, and his heartbeat slowed down. He inspected the thicket carefully, then looked at what he could see of the sky.

He took a bearing toward the swamp, following the growth of swamp maple and cypress. When it thinned out, he turned back, hoping to find Arcadie and Willie Tiger along the edge of the swamp. Twigs and dead branches snapped under his feet, and once he thought he heard an echoing snap far behind. He forced himself to call out, "Arcadie? Willie Tiger?"

There was no answer. He pushed through clumps of pickerelweed and bulrushes. Water splashed under his feet. He took a deep breath and smelled burning cloth. "Thank you, Lord," he whispered fervently, and hurried forward.

The bee tree stood in the shallow water like a sentinel, a thin pencil of smoke trickling from the top. No one was there. Even the horses were gone. Stunned, Josh clawed at the branch where Midnight had been tied. A few crushed leaves lay on the ground. He followed the hoof prints to the thick carpet of pine needles, then lost them.

Josh took a deep breath to quell the panic that threatened to overcome him. Then he measured with his eyes the beeline that would take him back to the camp. He started walking.

When he got to the myrtle thicket, he set his jaw and started down. The thickness of the growth forced him to pick his way as they had done earlier. Hopefully, he looked for hoof prints to point the way, but he realized he might be a few feet either to the left or the right of where they had passed earlier.

Once he stopped to look over his shoulder. Although he realized the trembling of the branches might have come from his own passing, he quickened his steps. When he reached the top of the ravine and the pines, he was almost running again.

The scent of charred ashes brought him up short. He looked around at the rough pine bough shelter, the protecting rocks that circled the ashes. He kicked at them with his foot. They were still warm. He had run right into a camp that was cleverly hidden in the pines.

Underbrush crackled behind him. Josh began to run. Tree trunks loomed out of the brush, and he dodged his way among them. Behind him, he heard the thudding of a galloping horse. His breath came in ragged gasps. Suddenly the pounding was right upon him. An arm scooped him up roughly and tumbled him across a saddle horn.

Josh kicked and thrashed out with his arms, screaming.

"Ow! Quit it, boy!" The voice was insistent and familiar.

"Arcadie?"

"Hold on, Josh. We've got to get out of here quick," Arcadie said. He urged his horse faster. The trees flashed by, their branches reaching for Josh's hair. He shrank back against Arcadie.

After a while, Arcadie slowed the pace of the big horse. Josh sat up stiffly. "Where's Midnight? What about the honey? Where's Willie Tiger? What happened back there?"

"Willie Tiger's at the edge of the woods. He's got the horses, and he's waiting on us. Forget about the honey." Arcadie's voice was rough. "We're not going back in there."

"Why? What was it?"

"Rustlers, probably. Outlaws," Arcadie half-answered. "Who knows?"

Willie Tiger saw them before they reached him. He met them, holding Midnight's reins. Still shaken, Josh mounted and followed them into the open. The sunlit grass lay before him like a placid pasture, safe as home. A mile away he saw the wagon drawn up near the river. The small figure near the tent would be Ma, and the rider would be Pa.

Suddenly he wanted to be with his father. He kicked Midnight and galloped toward the rider. Eben stopped and waited for him to catch up. He took one look at Josh and asked, "What happened?"

Josh had told most of it by the time Arcadie and Willie Tiger arrived. They filled in the rest. Pa gazed thoughtfully at the dark line of trees.

"We'll move out now," he said. "Help pack up, then meet us back here."

All through the short time it took to pack, Josh watched the line of trees. Nothing moved, nothing changed. The green sea was as peaceful as ever.

Whips cracking, the riders started the cattle moving. They headed south, toward the Caloosahatchee. By midday of the next morning, nothing had happened. Far behind them, the dark trees seemed to float, halfway between grass and sky.

After he had eaten the noon meal and lay warming in the sun, Josh felt the tension leave his body. Everyone relaxed; they seemed to feel that the incident might have been partly imagination. Everyone except Arcadie, who sat cleaning his gun.

And Daniel, who neither watched the horizon nor listened to the others, sat, eyes unseeing, and listened to the wind, the ground, and the birds. "They come," he said. "Five men, maybe six. Maybe more."

Eben put his cup down slowly. Arcadie stood up. They stared back towards the distant trees. There was no one in sight.

"When?" Eben asked.

"I don't know."

Eben looked at Arcadie. The thin man nodded and headed for his horse. "Keep the wagon moving, Penny," Eben said. "Willie Tiger, Josh, back to the herd."

For days they kept the cattle moving. Each night the old man shook his head. Another day on the trail followed, then another. Finally, they reached the Caloosahatchee and turned west. They slowed down, knowing the cattle had to graze before heading into the sand hill country. They took turns riding night watch. In the dead of the night, Josh still felt the familiar feathering along his neck and was grateful for the presence of Moki on watch.

So the days passed. And the nights.

Chapter Nine
High Wind

The wind came out of the west at dawn. It blew steadily, bringing with it the taste of rain. The sky never brightened that day or the next but stayed a leaden gray.

The riders carried canvas ponchos strapped to their saddles, but the rain didn't come. Although Daniel took to his bedroll in the wagon and both Arcadie and Eben complained, Josh enjoyed the feel of the damp air on his skin. After the heat of early July, the coolness was welcome. Even Penny, who had been stuck in the ovenlike wagon the past few weeks, didn't mind the change in the weather at first.

But the days passed, and the dampness began to cling to everything. The saddles felt clammy; even Josh's skin began to have a damp, fishy smell. The cook fire hissed and sputtered in the wind, and Penny fussed about it like a mother hen, trying to get the food to cook properly. Sometimes she lost the battle, and they were served meat burned on one side and half-raw on the other.

One look at Penny's frustrated face quenched any complaints. The food was eaten in tactful silence. Often, Josh tucked his half-eaten meat under his poncho to give to Moki. Then the riders disappeared back to the herd.

They found it easier to ride in the blustery air than to sit under the stifling tent.

"I just sat down to pull off my boot," Arcadie complained, "and my hands mildewed."

The unseen stalkers were forgotten in the general gloom that settled over the camp. Josh had never seen his mother depressed before. She began reading the Bible aloud to dispel her mood. "Can't be a gloomygus while you're listening to God's Word," she had always said. Josh knew many of the passages by heart. He took to reciting them to the cattle, enjoying the silken roll and thunder of the verses.

Daniel liked them too. When Penny's usually sunny mood broke through again, she began to wrap the Bible carefully to protect it from mildew before putting it away. Daniel protested. "Read more," he said.

Josh would ride in to find them together on the wagon seat, Bible open. Penny's lilting voice as she read kept Ornery moving slowly. The damp had settled the dust, and the two riders were able to talk comfortably about what Penny read. Seeing them reminded Josh of the little cabin, where Ma had taught him to read from the Bible. He rode away without interrupting them, taking the warm glow of memory back with him.

The rain came late in the week. It began in the night, drumming on the canvas tent. Josh woke and yawned, glad he wasn't on watch. Moki crawled into the tent and settled down next to Josh. Willie Tiger turned over. Josh looked up to see the Indian boy glaring, eyes hard, tense with anger. Willie Tiger called sharply in his own language. Moki sprang up and lay down beside the older boy.

Josh shrugged and turned his back. *I can't help it if Moki likes me,* he thought resentfully, pushing back memories of feeding the dog and playing with him while he was on watch. *A dog needs a friend too, not a—a—gloomygus!*

It rained steadily for days. Everything dripped. When the rain wasn't dripping, the wind sprayed it into every corner of the tent. The canvas threatened to become a sail. On the prairie, the water soaked the ground and began to stand in puddles. The puddles became larger and merged until the prairie was a shallow lake. Only the blades of wire grass emerging from the surface indicated that the cattle were walking on ground, not water. There was no place dry enough to sleep. They crowded into the wagon in shifts, trying to get enough rest to keep going. Nerves frayed, sometimes snapped.

Josh often took Moki with him when he rode herd. From the beginning, the catch dog had been shared with the riders. His job was to herd the cattle, and it didn't matter who was riding. This time, Josh didn't remember that Willie Tiger was riding, too. Carelessly, he whistled, calling Moki from Willie Tiger's side.

The dog wagged his tail and trotted after Josh. Willie Tiger shouted, but neither dog nor boy responded. Josh started out to get Midnight, Moki at his heels. Penny's cry alerted him. He looked up to see Willie Tiger charging him. The next thing he knew, he was in the mud, and Willie Tiger was on top of him. Instinctively, Josh began to fight. The two boys rolled over and over, punching wildly until Eben got hold of Josh, and Arcadie hauled Willie Tiger to his feet.

"Moki is my dog!" Willie Tiger said defiantly. "And you are trying to take him away!"

"Is that true, son?" Eben looked at Josh seriously, knowing how much he wanted a dog.

Josh glared back at Willie Tiger. He almost yelled, "Well, you're trying to take my pa!" but his lips clamped down over the words and they were never spoken.

"No, I'm not," he replied, as defiant as Willie Tiger. "Moki likes me, that's all."

Willie Tiger looked at him but said nothing else. He jerked away from Arcadie. Mounting his horse, he rode into the rain. Moki whined and followed.

Slowly Eben released his hold. "It's not like Willie Tiger to accuse you without reason," he said. "Are you sure you're telling the truth?"

"I knew you'd take his side!" Josh cried. "He's nothing! He's nothing but a dumb Injun!" He turned and blundered into Penny. Her appalled look sent him lunging out, away from the camp.

He walked for a while, but there was nowhere to go. Water covered every inch of the land. He straightened his shoulders and turned around. Kicking water with every step, he marched back to camp and saddled Midnight. No one spoke as he rode out to the herd.

At noon, everyone was silent. Eben and Penny were disturbed over the fight, Arcadie was obviously on Josh's side, and the old man watched them from the safety of his blanket. Willie Tiger barely ate and left the fire quickly, taking Moki with him.

The next day the rain ended, but the wind still blew from the west. They welcomed the sun with shouts of joy. Even Willie Tiger's mood lightened, and he came out to stand with the others. Between the sunshine and the wind, the water dried up rapidly. No damage seemed to have been done. If anything, the grass was greener than ever.

The wind continued without abating. About a week later, a black cloud appeared low on the southern horizon.

"Get blankets, mosquito netting," Daniel Ogalla told them. "Wrap face with netting, cover body with blankets. Cover nostrils of horses."

"Mosquitos?" Arcadie said unbelievingly. "Looks like more rain."

"Mosquitos. Lots of mosquitos," Daniel insisted.

"He's never been wrong," Eben said. "Penny, Josh, do as he says."

Arcadie watched the cloud uneasily. "Can we outrun it?"

"You can try." Daniel was not optimistic.

They bundled up as Daniel had said. As they rode to move the cows, Josh looked at the others in amazement. They looked like monsters out of a childish nightmare. Netting covered their hats and was tucked down inside their shirts. Blankets hunched over their backs and covered their clothing. *We look like huge bugs,* he thought. *It's a wonder we don't spook the cattle ourselves.*

Popping the whips, they got the cattle moving into the wind. When the mosquitos arrived, the herd was on the fringe of the cloud, with the wind blowing strongly. Still, in the first few minutes the herd disappeared into the cloud. Horrified, Josh saw the nose and mouth of a cow completely covered with a black mass of tiny insects. She fell to the ground.

Then thousands of mosquitos pelted against the netting that covered his face, stinging even through the net. Beside him, Moki went wild, barking shrilly. Tears streaming down his face, Josh kept cracking the whip, running toward the wind. The wind whipped the mass from the netting and he could see. Twice he had to dodge fallen cattle; then suddenly it was over. He looked back to see the swarm disappearing in a northeasterly direction.

All around him cows staggered blindly. The ground was littered with fallen cattle. One look told him the cows weren't going anywhere. He rode back to the wagon. Ornery stood drooping in the harness, head sagging. Penny and Daniel huddled in the wagon. Penny was moaning.

"Ma! Are you all right?" Josh started as she removed the net. Her eyes were puffy, and her hands were swollen where she had exposed them to clutch the net.

"I'll be fine," she said from between clenched teeth. "I just feel like I'm on fire. Oh, Josh!" She stared as he removed his net.

"I think we all look like this," Josh said, rubbing his face. He got down and took the netting off Midnight's nostrils while Penny released it from Ornery's broad muzzle. "You should see the cows. The mosquitos blocked their nostrils and mouths so they couldn't breathe. They went down like rocks."

Eben rode up and dismounted wearily. "If Daniel hadn't told us what to do, we'd have done the same. That, and if the good Lord hadn't kept that wind blowin'—" His voice trailed off, and he turned to stare out at the littered plain. "I won't give up, Penny," he said fiercely. "I won't give up."

Penny went to stand beside him, leaning against him. "I know. And I wouldn't want you to. We'll make it, Eben. I promise."

Eben gave her a wry smile at the echo of his own words. "I'll have to give the others a chance to leave, Penny. It's our battle, not theirs. From what we have left out there, we'd be truly blessed to make more than a few hundred dollars."

Arcadie and Willie Tiger straggled in and collapsed on the grass beside the wagon wheels. They looked no better than the others. They listened blankly as Eben explained the situation and gave them a choice to leave or stay.

Arcadie was the first to speak. "Miz Penny can still cook, can't she? I signed on for the whole trip, Eben Bramlett. You can't get rid of a broken-down cowpoke like me, first trouble that comes up. Arcadie men are tougher'n dry meat. I doubt if those little mosquitos got enough out of me to quench their thirst."

Josh grinned, then groaned as his face burned. Willie Tiger looked up at him, then at Eben. "It is for my grandfather to say," he replied, "but we are no strangers to trouble."

"We stay," Daniel agreed, "but your loss may not be so great as you think. Look."

Some of the "dead" cows were struggling to their feet. Eben stared at them incredulously. Then he shouted gleefully, "Clean 'em out, boys! Clean 'em out!"

The rest of the day was spent in cleaning masses of dead mosquitos out of the nostrils of the downed cows. It helped most, but others were too far gone. When they finished, the count was two hundred and fifty dead.

"Better than I thought, anyway," Eben said. He looked around the littered plain. Vultures were already circling overhead. "Let's take what we can for meat and clear out. This is a slaughterhouse."

When they got the herd moving, Josh rode alongside his father. "Pa, I'm proud that you aren't giving up."

"We're going to make it, son."

"I know, Pa." He hesitated for a minute. "I didn't expect everybody to stick with us, when it looked so bad. Why do you think they stayed?"

"Well, time spent in close quarters the way we have for the past few months will make you truly friends or enemies. I think, different as we are, we're becoming friends."

"Weren't we friends before?"

"In a way. But friendship can grow and deepen when friends share misfortunes, or it can wither into nothing. It's like our relationship with the Lord. It grows when we seek His company in prayer and trust in Him. It withers when we turn to others instead."

Josh took a deep breath. "I'm sorry I yelled at you the other day. And that I didn't apologize right away. If anything had happened, I would never have forgiven myself."

"You've been forgiven, son. But what about Willie Tiger? He really thought you were trying to take his dog."

"I was." Josh spoke quietly but bluntly. "I fed him. He likes me, Pa, maybe even better than he likes Willie Tiger."

"Still, he belongs to someone else. Stealing affection is stealing, plain and simple."

"I know, Pa. I'll talk to him."

Admitting his guilt to Willie Tiger and asking forgiveness was the hardest thing Josh had ever done in his life. Willie Tiger's face showed no emotion, and his eyes were carefully shadowed. Josh finished and started to walk away.

"Wait."

Josh turned back, surprised.

"Why do you tell me this?"

"Because it's the truth," Josh replied, puzzled.

"I have known that," Willie Tiger said. "I mean, why do you admit wrong to me?"

"You mean because you're an Indian?" Josh asked.

Willie Tiger nodded.

"That makes no difference to God, nor to us either," Josh said. "Wrong is wrong, no matter who it gets done to."

Silently, Willie Tiger rubbed Moki behind the ears as he had seen Josh do. Josh watched for a few minutes, but Willie Tiger showed no desire to continue the conversation. He walked away, leaving the boy with his dog.

Chapter Ten
An Owl Speaks

Arcadie herded the strays away from the woods and back into the open. For days he had been quiet and had kept to himself. If Josh had not considered the idea so ridiculous, he would have said Arcadie's appetite had fallen off.

"Somethin's wrong with Arcadie," he told his father. "Do you know what it is?"

"Maybe he has a bellyache like you had last spring," Eben said, grinning. Then his face sobered. "I'm a little more worried about Daniel. "

Josh understood. Daniel had never recovered from the mosquito bites. They had brought on another attack of malaria, and he lay in the wagon, burning with fever.

Penny nursed him, but this time she told Eben that the old man was too frail. She didn't think he would make it through. She was honest with Willie Tiger, too. Eben sent the boy back to the wagon to help Penny and to be with his grandfather.

Willie Tiger woke Josh at the first watch. "You take Moki," he said.

Josh stared. Since the trouble with Willie, he had been careful to stay away from the dog.

"You take him," Willie Tiger insisted. He left the tent, leaving the dog with Josh.

Josh hugged the shaggy dog, rubbing the hair along his back. "You need a bath," he said. Moki wagged his tail.

Moki went with him every night, trotting at Midnight's heels. The herd was bunched together in the dark, and the dog's services weren't really needed, but his company was. Josh talked to him constantly as he rode. Moki was with him when he saw the rider.

At first he thought it was Arcadie. The height and build were about the same, and the big horse resembled Arcadie's in the dark. The rider was sitting on his horse, not moving, looking out over the herd as if it were his own. Josh galloped up, glad to have early relief on the watch. Moki's rumble warned him too late.

The rider's horse wheeled, and Josh saw the hooknose and the scar high on the cheekbone. Moonlight glinted off the barrel of a pistol, and eyes that seemed to stare a hole through Josh gleamed in the dark. Unable to move, Josh closed his eyes for a moment, expecting a bullet to put a real hole through his chest.

Moki sprang forward and was clubbed down with the pistol. Then the darkness swallowed up the rider as if he had never been. Only the hoof beats of his galloping horse told Josh that what he had seen was real. Shivering, he called Moki back and rode around the herd.

Arcadie was on the other side, humming softly to himself. When Josh described the rider, he felt Arcadie stiffen. For the first time, Josh noticed the rifle in Arcadie's hand.

"You probably saw a drifter. Just lookin' us over," Arcadie said quietly. "Go on back to camp and get your pa. We'll finish watch."

"But, Arcadie—"

"Go on, boy." Arcadie's voice was grim, and Josh obeyed.

For the next few nights, Josh wasn't allowed to ride watch. Instead, he stayed at the wagon with the others. He chafed at the restriction and wished he had never told Arcadie about the rider.

Willie Tiger's concern was for his grandfather. Josh could hardly get two words out of him. Penny was busy with the cooking and nursing Daniel. Moki was with the herd.

The days weren't bad, for he was allowed to come and go as he wished. The nights were different. It was late July, and the nights were hot. The tent that provided sanctuary during the day became an oven at night. Josh moved his bedroll out into the open. Above him the sky hung like an umbrella, soft and velvety. From its ribs hung golden stars, dangling almost within his reach.

His father joined him one night after watch. "You still awake, Josh?"

"Yes, sir," Josh replied, rolling over to make room for Eben.

Eben stretched out beside Josh, groaning a little as his tired muscles relaxed. "Purty, aren't they? Look, there's the big Bear and its cub." Eben pointed, tracing the imaginary lines between the stars with his finger.

"And there's the Archer." Josh pointed out his favorite constellation of the hunter and his dog.

"Speaking of dogs," Eben said as he sat up, "how are you and Willie Tiger getting along lately?"

"Okay, I reckon." Josh stared up at the sky. "He's with Daniel mostly. Pa?"

"Uh-huh?"

"What happens when a person dies?"

"If they are saved, their soul goes to heaven to be with Jesus. You know that, son."

"I mean, what happens to them here?"

"You mean their body?"

"Yes." Josh turned over to look at his father. "I never saw anybody die. Or even seen a body dead."

"Death comes to 'most everything the same. Remember the little squirrel you tried to raise once?"

Josh nodded. "His heart stopped beating, and he got real limp. Then later on he was stiff."

"It's the same with all God's creatures. When the life leaves the body, it just stops."

Josh moved restlessly. "If Daniel believes an owl is calling him instead of Jesus, what will happen to his soul?"

Eben rubbed his son's shoulder. "Your ma has had a lot of time with Daniel in that wagon. If anybody can get a man to see the light, your ma can. She won't let go until the last breath is gone, Josh."

Josh didn't say anything for a while. He lay on the blanket, thinking about the faith of his parents. He tried to put himself in Willie Tiger's place, with no father, no mother, and a dying grandfather. A pang of sympathy shot through him.

"What will happen to Willie Tiger?"

"He'll have us, Josh. I've tried to be something of a father to him, and your ma would be glad of another child to mother. We Bramletts have plenty of love to go around."

Josh bent his head, ashamed. He hoped his father never guessed how he really felt about Willie Tiger.

"But I reckon he'll head on south to find his relatives. I know that's what I would do in his place. I'd want to be with my kin." He stood up stiffly. "Well, goodnight partner. I'll check on your ma."

"Goodnight, Pa."

For a long time, Josh lay awake, thinking about his family. The days in the little cabin seemed years away. He tried to imagine the family home, blocking out the existence of his new friends one by one. He found he wouldn't want to go back to just three Bramletts. The lives of Arcadie, Daniel, and even Willie Tiger had become woven into the strands of his own life. The thought of losing any of them started a slow ache in his heart.

When the morning came and Penny told him Daniel had died in his sleep, Josh had already done his grieving. He was glad it had happened so easily for Daniel.

Then he asked slowly, "Did he answer the owl?"

"No, Josh," Penny gave him a quick hug. "He accepted Christ as his Saviour yesterday afternoon. I'm sorry. Your pa told me about your concern last night. I was so busy, I didn't take time to tell you, and when I came out here, you were already asleep."

Josh let out his breath. "How's Willie Tiger?"

"It's hard to tell. He's quiet as usual." Penny sighed. "I hate to see a child hold so much pain inside. It's not good. I wish you'd get close to him, Josh. Help him."

"I don't know how, Ma." Josh was troubled. *It was hard enough to talk to Willie Tiger about everyday things. How could he talk about things that really mattered?* he thought.

"Just be his friend," Penny said. "The time will come."

They buried Daniel on a rise near the woods. Eben read from the Bramletts' Bible, rejoicing that Daniel was in heaven and no longer endured the trials of this earth.

Arcadie turned his hat over and over in his hands, creasing the rim. He shifted his feet awkwardly, watching first one, then the other. Josh met his eyes, and Arcadie looked down.

Josh was puzzled. He had never seen Arcadie so uncomfortable. He glanced at Willie Tiger. The boy stood straight and tall, as if he had passed from a child into a man overnight. He did not cry, but he remained at the grave long after the others had gone.

Josh had expected Willie Tiger to be angry and more withdrawn than ever. Instead, Willie Tiger seemed to become stronger. Josh remembered his mother's desire with amazement. This new Willie Tiger didn't need help. In his presence, Josh felt like a child.

Arcadie was different too. It was as if the passing of Daniel affected them all. No longer did Arcadie treat Willie Tiger with contempt. Willie Tiger became a real person, not just an "Injun" as Arcadie had viewed him before. Josh tried to put a name to the difference in Arcadie's treatment of Willie Tiger. It wasn't love, nor even friend-ship. After mulling it over in his mind, he settled on respect. Arcadie was showing respect.

The discovery didn't ease Josh's disturbance any. If anything, he felt the two years difference between himself and Willie Tiger more keenly. Josh was well acquainted with his own reactions. He knew he would have cried, for he rushed into most situations rashly. With his heart on his sleeve, his mother said. This time, he was determined to be as grown-up as Willie Tiger. Taking his cue from the older boy, he tightened his rein on his emotions and began to emulate Willie Tiger's newfound confidence.

Chapter Eleven
River Crossing

"It's time to move on."

Eben spoke the words gently. Willie Tiger flinched, and Josh saw the first crack in the boy's confidence.

"When?"

"By first light," Eben replied. "We need to be in Punta Rassa two weeks from now."

Willie Tiger nodded. "I'll be ready."

When the boy slipped away from the tent, Josh followed. Only he knew that Willie Tiger visited Daniel's grave every day. He couldn't say what made him want to invade the boy's privacy. A taut, hard knot inside his chest and a burning lump in his throat drove him on.

For the first time in his life, he was at a loss for words. He stood beside Willie Tiger at the grave, sharing in his grief silently. He didn't know who cried first, but he guessed it was himself. And he knew he was crying for more than Daniel. He cried for himself and for Willie Tiger, for the anger and the guilt of the last five months. When it was over, he felt clean. Willie Tiger met his eyes without speaking, and Josh knew he felt the same way.

The next morning, they packed up at dawn. The familiar cracking of whips started the cattle moving, stirring dust from the trampled grass. Josh looked back over the waving blades of yellow. From this distance, the mound of dirt could have been the shadow of a pine.

They kept the cattle moving for a few days, before setting up camp again near the river. Everyone knew this would be the last camp before reaching Punta Rassa. Even this far inland, the air held a scent of salt. Occasionally a straying seagull would dive for scraps from Penny's cooking pot.

Grazing was sparse, even along the river. The cows took to stripping the foliage off the brush. They were heavy, some ponderously so. Counting in the new calves, Eben reckoned they were only a hundred shy of the number that had begun the drive.

"Gold on the hoof," he chuckled, allowing his spirits to rise as his goal came closer. His elation infected the others, and a spirit of excitement reigned in the camp.

"We'll cross the river tomorrow," Eben told them. "This is as shallow a spot as I've seen yet. Don't know what it'll be like downstream."

Penny got up and walked to the river's edge. She stared silently across to the other bank. Eben joined her. They walked for a while along the riverbank.

"There's a ferry downriver, Pen. I'll never make you ford a river," Eben promised. "I know you're afraid of water."

Penny laughed shakily. "Should have learned to swim long ago," she said, "but I just couldn't bring myself to trust the water to hold me up."

"You'd float like a feather," Eben teased, picking her up. He carried her back to the camp, with her protesting all the way.

"Aw, Pa," Josh grumbled, embarrassed at the way his parents were carrying on in front of Willie Tiger.

Eben laughed and put Penny down. She flounced under the tent, pretending to be in a huff. Eben tweaked Josh's ear. "You didn't used to be so easily embarrassed."

He looked around. "Where's Arcadie?"

"He rode out a while ago," Willie Tiger said. "He said he had business to take care of."

"In Punta Rassa?" Eben frowned.

Josh stared at Willie Tiger in surprise. Without Arcadie, they'd be short-handed for the crossing.

"North," was Willie Tiger's answer.

Josh stood up to look along the back trail. The sand hills stretched into the distance. He tried to distinguish a rider from the clumps of saw-toothed palmettos and Spanish bayonet, but nothing moved in the shimmering heat.

"Let it go," Eben told him, clapping the boy on the shoulder. "Arcadie'll be back when he's ready."

That afternoon, Willie Tiger and Josh located a bed of shellcrackers in the bullrushes. They sharpened sticks for spears and waded out into the shallow water. Their first efforts muddied the water, but so many of the yellow-bellied fish squirmed and splashed in the reeds that they finally speared enough for Penny's frying pan.

Arcadie came riding in as the scent of frying fish rose into the air. He followed the smell to Penny's fire. "I always know how to bring you in." Penny smiled as he filled his plate. "Where've you been, anyway?"

"Just ridin'," he replied. "Thought I saw a homestead back yonder aways. I been hankerin' for some fresh aiggs."

Eben held out his plate to be filled. "Couple of days and you can have all the eggs you can hold. I'm gonna take you all to the best restaurant in Punta Rassa. We'll eat until we're full."

They bunched the cattle for the night, and left Moki with them. Eben wanted them to be together for a while. "We took turns ridin' watch so long, I doubt if we've done much more than pass and repass for the last few weeks. Arcadie, me and Pen want to thank you for the job you've done for us. We couldn't have done without you. Nor you, Willie Tiger. But beyond that, you've become family. You'll both be welcome at our fireside any day."

Josh watched as Arcadie stared down at his boots. Willie Tiger met Eben's eyes and smiled. The firelight softened the planes of his face and warmed his dark eyes. Josh thought back over the last months. Troubled, he realized that while Willie Tiger had relaxed and become more outgoing, Arcadie had withdrawn. His gaze went from one to the other as Eben continued.

"And you know how much help Daniel was."

For a moment they were silent, remembering Daniel's ability to sense trouble before it arrived. Josh wished he were still with them. Penny dispelled the solemn mood by producing a skillet full of crispy turnovers. "I've been savin' a jar of dewberry jam for four months," she said, laughing as they reached eagerly for the hot pies.

Josh forgot about his worries and bit into the flaky crust, licking at the sweet jam that ran down his chin. The others followed his example, and the feeling of celebration returned.

The next morning, Arcadie and Willie Tiger stayed with the herd while Josh and his father took Penny to the ferry. Midnight and the big gray were hitched behind the wagon. Eben drove the wagon, and Penny sat beside him. Josh took his usual place behind the seat, surprised that he no longer had to stand to see past his parents.

The ferry was a thick-planked, square barge. Ropes that passed through iron rings on the barge stretched from one bank to the other. The ferryman accepted their coins, turning them over in his hand.

"Sorry, folks," he said, nodding to Penny, "but you'd be surprised at what some fools try to pass off on me."

"Many people come this way?"

"Nope. And a lot of them swim the river when they find out what the fare is. Folks around here don't have much cash money. You headed for Punta Rassa?"

Eben nodded as Josh climbed out to hold Ornery's harness. "We're taking my wife over; then me and my boy'll come back and get the herd."

"Cost extry." The man spat in the river.

"Eben! I could have managed by myself," Penny said with distress.

"Don't fret," Eben told her. "I promised I'd see you over. And, just like the man said, me and Josh can swim back over."

Mollified, she settled back on the seat, keeping her eyes off the river. "Is it deep?"

The ferryman shook his head. "Never seen anybody have trouble crossing. I usually get the wagons, or maybe somebody who don't like gettin' wet."

Ornery pulled them up the other bank without much effort. They creaked along the river, heading back upstream where the cattle waited. When they were opposite the herd, Eben stopped the wagon under the shade of a turkey oak. Then he and Josh mounted and rode down the bank.

The horses splashed into the water, kicking up spray in the shallows. Then the water deepened, and Josh sensed the shift of balance when Midnight's feet left the bottom. He felt a jolt of alarm; then the small horse struck out against the current, swimming strongly. A few feet away he saw his father, wet to the waist as the big gray churned the water.

Willie Tiger and Arcadie saw them coming and shouted encouragement from the far bank. When the horses got their footing and surged up the bank, they all shouted.

"It'll be an easy crossing," Eben told them. "It's not really deep here. Boys, keep the cattle moving and don't give them a chance to panic. If one goes down, get out of its way. Don't risk your own life."

They unfurled the eighteen-foot bullwhips and got the herd moving. The cattle poured down the bank and into the water, bawling and scattering dust. Once in the water, they swam easily. Two riders on either side kept them going in a straight line from one bank to the other. It took over two hours to get the herd across and round up the few stragglers. By then the line of cattle stretched out over a quarter mile, still moving together. The dust raised from their passing forced Josh to cover his mouth with a square of cloth. He brought his whip around in a circle and cracked it out its full length. This was a cattle drive!

Looking back, Josh saw Penny and Ornery fall in behind the herd, but no other figures were distinguishable in the thick dust but the cattle. He didn't see the others until dusk, when the herd was circled for the night.

The next few days passed in a blue haze. Each day was the same, hot and choked with dust. Josh wiped his face with a little water from his canteen, thankful that they hadn't tried to drive the cattle this way straight from Kissimmee. In the second week, they circled the cattle a few miles outside of Punta Rassa.

Eben took Josh in with him to make the sale. Josh heard the ocean before he saw it. The air was tangy with salt, and seagulls like the ones that sometimes raided the camp glided overhead, screeching. Salt-burned palmettos marched along the ridges of sand. Spanish bayonet and sea grape struggled for a hold on the sliding dunes. At the top of a sand hill they stopped to stare at the booming surf in wonder.

"There's enough water for Ma to bathe all the children in the world," Josh said wonderingly. "Look, you can't tell where water ends and sky begins. Ain't it a marvel?"

"It's one of the wonders of creation," Eben agreed. "Your ma'll love it. Maybe we can stay a few days. If Kissimmee has a hotel, this place is bound to have one."

Reluctantly Josh tore his gaze from the shimmering ocean and shaded his eyes. Down to the right, buildings crowded almost to the water's edge. Holding pens backed the buildings and, on the waterfront, a wharf stretched a hundred feet into the surf. Out in the bay, two steamers lay at anchor. The wind changed, bringing the smell of cattle.

"We're in the right place," Eben said, wrinkling his nose. "Let's see if we can sell the yellowhammers."

They rode slowly into town, inspecting each building as they passed it. The weathered gray buildings contained a post office and cafe, a general merchandise store, saloon, livery stable, feed store and blacksmith shop. Eben had begun to worry when Josh pointed out a two-story clapboard house whose sign read "Rooms to Rent."

They turned down the dirt road leading to the waterfront and stopped in front of a store. An old man rocked on the porch.

"We have cattle for sale," Eben called. "Who do we see?"

The old man spit tobacco and waved a hand toward the wharf. "You're headed in the right direction. The Cap'n's in that shack on the dock."

Josh and Eben rode down to the dock. They dismounted and tied their horses to a hitching rail. Then Eben took a deep breath and straightened his shirt.

"This is it, partner," he said. He knocked on the weathered door of the shack.

"Come in, door's open," a voice called.

Eben pushed the door open and stood back for Josh to enter first. Two men sat on stools near a salt-encrusted window, writing in ledgers. Another man, tall and about fifty, sat in a rocking chair, his outstretched legs encased in leather boots.

His amused gaze took in Josh's bare feet and overalls, then met Eben's eyes.

"We're lookin' for the Cap'n," Eben said firmly. "We have cattle for sale."

The man came to his feet with outstretched hand. "They call me Captain," he said, "and I'm buying. You run those cattle down from the scrub?"

"No," Eben replied. "We took our time and grazed them on the way. They'll run five hundred each, easy."

The man gave him a look of respect. "I see you know cattle. Most folks run yellowhammers down here and try to sell us walking skeletons. If you're right about the pounds, they'll go top dollar. And right now that's sixteen dollars a head."

Josh's head spun. Sixteen dollars a head, for over eight hundred scrub cows! Frantically, he tried to remember what Ma had taught him about figuring. That was over twelve thousand dollars!

Vaguely, he heard his father make arrangements to bring the cattle in. Then he followed him out, his bare feet stumbling on the porch step. They mounted without speaking, and rode slowly through the town, encased in a bubble of shock, joy, anticipation, and who knows what else. Only at the ridge of the sand hill did they dare look at one another.

Eben began to laugh, and Josh joined in almost hysterically. Then, whooping and laughing and scaring every creature within miles, they galloped the horses full out back to the camp.

Chapter Twelve
Gold on the Hoof

"Don't you shake one pound off those cows," Eben warned them when they started out the next day. "They're worth their weight in gold."

By ten o'clock the stream of cattle had poured over the ridge and was herded down into the holding pens. The Captain met Eben at the pens with several of his men. Eben watched confidently as they counted the herd. The final tally was eight hundred and forty-two. Eben signed the tally and motioned for Josh to follow him back to the shack.

The Captain settled himself behind one of the desks and reached for pen and paper. "Top line beef, Mr. Bramlett," he said. "Sixteen's a good price."

Josh held his breath as the man figured quickly. He finished and pushed the paper across to Eben. "Eight hundred and forty-two at sixteen dollars a head comes to thirteen thousand four hundred and seventy-two dollars. We pay in Spanish gold, Mr. Bramlett. Do you have any way of carrying it?"

Eben cleared his throat twice. "A wagon. I'll have to buy a trunk. Can I come back and pick it up?"

"Sure, or you can take the bags with you. I've seen cattlemen drop bags holding twenty or thirty thousand in gold on the cafe porch. Nobody's gonna bother your gold here. It's too heavy to go on a horse, and you could run down a wagon in less than a mile."

The Captain opened his safe and pulled out heavy bags. He grunted as he lifted them to the table. "There's twenty-seven bags of gold. Each one holds five hundred dollars, with the last one short some, of course."

Eben stared at the mass of bags. "Can I just take the short one and come back for the rest?"

"Sure. You just enjoy your meal. I'll be here all day."

Eben hefted the bag over his shoulder. Then he and Josh went to find the wagon. He gave Arcadie, Willie Tiger, and Josh gold coins and told them to meet him at the cafe. "We'll pick up the rest later. Unless you want your share now?"

Both Willie Tiger and Arcadie shook their heads. "We can wait."

"Then I'll get us a place to sleep. See you at the cafe at noon, boys."

Leaving Moki with the wagon and the others to their own plans, he and Penny walked across the street to the rooming house. It wasn't fancy, having been built to accommodate cattlemen, but it was clean.

"I'd like a room upstairs," Penny whispered to Eben. "Maybe we could look out over the ocean."

Eben booked a front upstairs room for himself and Penny after being assured that the ocean could be seen from the windows. Then he asked for a room for Arcadie and one for the boys. He paid for the rooms in gold, enjoying the feel of the smooth coin in his hand.

The clerk grinned. "First time in?"

Eben flushed. "Brought some cows from Kissimmee way. Sold them a while ago."

"You'll get used to it," the clerk said, tossing the coins into the register. "Most men make this drive once a year. Cattle flows one way, gold another. In betwixt," he added, eyes twinkling with satisfaction, "I manage to get a coin or two."

"Is there any place here to take a bath?" Penny asked, brushing at her skirt.

"Waal, we don't have many ladies," was the doubtful reply. "There's a bathhouse down near the stables."

At Penny's disappointed look, he thought a minute. "Miz Lunston, that runs the cafe, I hear tell she had a hip bath sent in. Maybe we can work something out."

"Thank you." Penny's face lit up with a relieved smile. "There hasn't been much real bathing on the trail."

"I'll see what I can do," he promised.

When they finished, it wasn't noon, so they walked down to the beach. Josh saw them and waved as they passed the general store. He was sitting out on the porch with Arcadie and Willie Tiger, eating crackers and cheese.

"You boys will ruin your dinner," Penny called.

"Don't count on it," Josh called back happily. "This salt air has me hungry as a bear the first of spring."

He and Willie Tiger had finished the crackers when Arcadie stood up suddenly. Josh saw his hand drop to his gun. He turned and saw five men riding down the dirt street. At first he thought he understood Arcadie's nervousness. They looked mean. Dirty and mean.

Then he saw the fourth one. He was tall and lean like Arcadie, with dark eyes and a thick scar across one cheek.

"Arcadie!" he said, excitedly. "It's the rider!"

His voice carried in the salt air. The rider reined in his horse and sat watching Josh. The other four ranged around him. For a moment, the jingling of bits and stamping of horses' hooves filled the deadly silence. Then the rider spoke. "Howdy, 'Cade."

Josh blinked. His breath caught in his throat as Arcadie answered evenly, "Howdy, Zack. What kept you?"

"A little business the other side of the river," the man replied, fingering his scar. His eyes left Josh and rested on Willie Tiger. "When'd you start keeping company with Injuns? There's no bounty on them now."

Arcadie's hand dropped lower. A rifle appeared over the pommel of one of the riders' saddles. Willie moved back into the shadows along the wall. Josh tried to follow, but his feet wouldn't move.

The rider's laughter rumbled hoarsely. "Not now, 'Cade. Not here."

The rifle slid back into its sheath. Leather creaked as the men reined their horses and headed for the saloon across the street. Josh watched numbly as they dismounted. They looked back across the street. One of them made a comment. Roaring with raucous laughter, they entered the saloon.

Josh stared at Arcadie. "Bounty hunter?"

Arcadie shrugged.

"You know those men!"

When Arcadie still didn't answer, Josh swung around to look for Willie Tiger. The Seminole boy was gone. Josh gave Arcadie one last furious stare and stalked away. Willie Tiger wasn't in the store, or the stables. Josh found him at the hardware store. Willie Tiger had thrown his coin on the counter and demanded a gun.

"I told you I could pay!" he told the gunsmith.

"Your money's no good here." The big man picked up the coin and flicked it back. It spun on end and clattered face down.

"It's gold!"

The man's face was stony. "And you're Seminole. We don't sell guns to Seminoles."

Willie Tiger picked up the coin and charged through the door, nearly knocking Josh down. "Wait, Willie!" he cried.

The boy slowed down long enough to yell at Josh, "Go away!" Then he turned down a dirt alleyway between the buildings. Josh followed, keeping out of range. Willie Tiger went on down to the dock and onto the wharf, moving as if he would charge right off the end into the water. Alarmed, Josh closed the distance between them. At the end, Willie Tiger suddenly sat down, swinging his legs above the water. His back was bent in defeat.

Josh sat down beside him. For a while he let Willie Tiger ignore him. Then he asked, "Who was the pistol for? Arcadie? Or the rider?"

"Both, I guess." Willie Tiger's voice was tired beyond his years. "Grandfather hoped that times would change before we got back. It was his dream—to live as he had before. His dream died with him."

"It didn't if it's yours too," Josh said quietly. "You make your dreams come true. Like Pa."

At the mention of Eben, Willie Tiger's face relaxed a little. "Your pa's not like other men."

"I know that. But there are other men who think like him." Josh pressed on. "Besides, you're special too." With sudden vision, he added, "And so am I."

Willie Tiger's eyes still held an unbelieving look. "And what about the riders?"

"There'll always be men like the riders. Men who live by preying on others."

"And Arcadie?"

Josh answered honestly. "I don't know whether Arcadie is a good one or a bad one. Maybe everybody can't be squeezed on one side or the other. I reckon we'll just have to wait and find out."

The other boy nodded. "That is fair."

Josh glanced at the sun. "It's time to meet Pa. He'll get it straightened out. Besides, there's nowhere else to go."

Willie Tiger accepted the logic of Josh's statement silently. The two boys made their way back to the cafe, avoiding the open saloon door. Arcadie was slouched in a rocking chair on the cafe porch, hat over his eyes. Penny and Eben waited on a bench, watching the boys with puzzled looks.

When they stepped onto the porch, Penny scolded, "You're late. Your pa's hungry. He didn't eat crackers and cheese like two boys I know."

Arcadie lifted his hat. His eyes met Josh's squarely. "I think we have something to take care of first."

Eben looked from one to the other. "We can talk inside."

They found a table in the back big enough to seat their group. When the waitress appeared, they asked for water and coffee.

"That all?" Her eyebrows raised.

"We need to talk a minute," Eben said, smiling at her. "Can we order later?"

"Sure, just wave and I'll come back."

Nobody said anything until Penny poured the coffee. Eben lifted his cup and drank appreciatively.

"Now," he said, putting the cup down. "What's going on?"

Josh and Willie Tiger looked at Arcadie. He rubbed his mustache, but didn't look down. "The riders followed us into town. I know them. I used to ride with one of them, down Arcadie way."

Penny gasped.

"The others come from Ten Thousand Islands, a rustler's roost down near Big Cypress Swamp. They're a mean bunch of men, and they're out for gold."

"How do you know this?" Eben stared at Arcadie as if he had sprouted a new set of ears.

"Down at the Caloosahatchee, before we crossed, I rode out to meet them. I knew they were still trailing us, and I wanted to know what they were after. It wasn't the cattle. Zack is waiting for you to start back through the wilderness with the gold."

"But they can't carry it," Eben argued. "The Cap'n said it was safe here, just laying on the porches."

"Here, maybe," Arcadie answered calmly. "But ten miles out, they'll kill you all and take your wagon. There'll be no chase from dead people. They can take all the time they want to reach the Islands with the gold on the wagon."

"Arcadie," Penny's eyes were huge in her white face. "Did you do these things too?"

Arcadie shook his head. "I rode with Zack back in the fifties, hunting Seminoles for bounty. That's all. I left him before he became what he is now."

"Bounty?" Penny's voice was faint.

"Yes'm." Arcadie looked across at Willie Tiger. "Didn't know any Injuns then. I was young and just doing a job. That's not much excuse, I guess. I haven't admitted to huntin' Injuns since. Even before I met you and Daniel. It's not somethin' I'm proud of."

"Anybody can make a mistake," Eben said slowly. "You didn't have to tell us. As far as I'm concerned, you're still my drover."

He looked around the table. Penny nodded, still pale. Willie Tiger's nod was barely noticeable.

Josh spoke up. "How do we know you're still not one of their gang?"

Arcadie looked at him impassively. "You'll just have to trust me."

After a minute, Josh nodded, hesitantly.

"Then that's that." Eben signaled for the waitress. "Bring us some of everything on the menu," he told her, "and keep it coming. I'm about to starve to death."

She giggled and departed, returning quickly with platters of fried chicken, shrimp, and clams. Bowls of greens and fresh fruit filled the center of the table.

Josh's appetite returned as the steaming food teased his nostrils. He ate until his stomach could hold no more. The only one who did not do justice to the food was Arcadie. When they finished, his plate held no more bones than Penny's plate. Josh saw and frowned, his suspicion returning. If confession was good for both the soul and the appetite, as Penny had often told him, it hadn't done much for Arcadie.

After the bill was paid, Eben took them over to the general merchandise store. He outfitted them with new jeans, shirts, and boots, topping everything off with broad-brimmed cattlemen's hats and red bandanas. "Might as well look the part, men," he said expansively. "The Bramlett and Son Cattle Company is on its way."

Josh beamed, wriggling his toes in the boots. He swaggered down the aisle, just to get the feel of them. They felt grand, even if they did pinch his toes a mite.

There was little in the store for women. "Don't have much call for women's stuff," the storekeeper said apologetically. "Maybe down in Fort Myers?"

Penny shook her head. "I have enough. Unless—do you know where I could get orange trees?"

"Sure," he answered, glad to find something for her. "We got some off the boat yesterday. We got them for a grower down in Fort Myers, but they always send a little extry. Might have about ten trees."

"We'll take them," Eben said eagerly.

Eben bought a trunk and picked up the rest of the money. It took two men to load it onto the wagon, where it stayed for the rest of the time they spent in Punta Rassa. He and Penny spent a lot of time on the beach, walking along the sand like youngsters.

After the first night of tossing back and forth in starched sheets, Josh and Willie Tiger used their room to store their new clothes. They took their bedrolls and Moki and moved out on the point, where they lay under the Australian pines. They swam in the ocean and fished in the blue and white coves. At night they ate red snapper and grouper grilled on a bed of hot coals. Sometimes Eben and Penny joined them for a night under the stars. Arcadie never came.

Chapter Thirteen
Ambush!

They left Punta Rassa the morning of the fifth day. Slipping out unseen was impossible. The wagon made enough noise to wake the dead, and on a good day, even a gopher could outrun Ornery. When they passed the saloon, the riders' horses were still there.

"Be a miracle if they can shoot straight," Josh muttered.

Arcadie's grin was grim. "I wouldn't count on liquor spoilin' their aim. They were weaned on it."

About a mile out of town, Eben stopped the wagon. He lifted the canvas on the back. Four rifles and three handguns lay in the folds, surrounded by boxes of shells. When he handed one of the rifles to Penny, Josh gasped. "Ma?"

"I can shoot if it's a choice between life or death, son," she said firmly. "Your pa and I knew we were movin' to the wilderness when we came here."

Willie Tiger took his eagerly, turning it over in his hand to inspect the gun's mechanism.

"Arcadie will show you how to shoot." Eben tossed the other rifle to Josh. "Or Josh. You'll need to protect yourself."

They watched Eben silently as he passed out the shells. "We could just find a good place and ambush them," he told them, "but that would leave us no better than they are. And it certainly wouldn't set well with anybody here. We'll try to avoid trouble if possible. Maybe we can hold them off. We have plenty of ammunition." He turned to Arcadie. "Arcadie has some suggestions."

"Our best defense is to be alert," Arcadie said. "Stay away from anything that would give them cover. My guess is they'll hit us upriver, past the ferry."

"Near where we camped before?"

"Yes. The only problem is that Zack knows me as well as I know him. And he always was full of surprises. A twisted mind, if I ever saw one. I'd be prepared for anything. Zack ain't a brave man. He relies on surprise and will cut his losses and run if he fails."

"Do you think we'll make it?" Josh asked.

"There's One who knows," Penny said softly.

Eben nodded. "Just finding them won't be hard. Getting through without losing any of us will take prayer."

He bent his head. Willie Tiger bowed his head, a look of peace and confidence on his face. Josh saw Arcadie bow his head, for once without embarrassment; then he closed his own eyes.

When the wagon rolled out, everyone moved with a sense of purpose. If fear plagued any of them, it was not visible. At the ferry, they crossed together with Moki at their heels.

The bond of danger encircled them, bringing them back into one closely knit group. When they camped at night, they didn't build a fire, but ate beef jerky by the light of the moon. They kept watch all night, taking turns as they had done with the cattle.

Josh found himself alone with Arcadie. The questions he had held in spilled over. "Why didn't you tell us before? And why did you keep to yourself at Punta Rassa?"

"Is it something you would've blurted out if it didn't need to be said? And did you really want me around then?" Arcadie's look was tired. "When this is over, we'll talk," he promised.

Josh had to be satisfied with his answer. The night passed and morning came. It was hot before dawn.

"It's going to be a scorcher," Penny said quietly. She filled their canteens from the water barrel. "We'd better fill the barrels back up in case we get pinned down somewhere."

Arcadie agreed. He and Eben lashed the barrels to the travois Daniel had built and started for the river. Josh rode with them, rifle ready. Willie Tiger and Moki stayed at the wagon with Penny.

Just as they started back with the barrels, they heard shots. Josh spurred Midnight and raced back, rifle ready. Arcadie thundered behind him. Eben kicked the gray into a gallop, splashing water as the travois bounced over the sand.

They found Moki lying on the ground. Willie Tiger and Penny came out from behind the wagon, rifles in hand. Willie Tiger ran to kneel beside Moki.

"What happened?" Josh slid off Midnight and squatted beside Willie Tiger. "Is he dead? Who fired?"

"They must have been watching us," Willie Tiger said. "When you went for water, they attacked. Moki warned us in time, but they shot him. They left him when they realized they hadn't surprised us."

"They'll be back," Arcadie said. "They want that gold."

Eben held Penny tightly. "All this for a few cows. If I had known this would endanger your lives, I'd have given it up. As a matter of fact, I feel like chucking that chest of gold out into the sand and leaving it there."

"It wouldn't do any good," Arcadie said. "They'd never believe you'd let them get away."

Eben sighed. "I know. We'd better get going. It's going to be a long day."

"What about Moki?" Josh asked, surprised that they had forgotten him in the excitement. Willie Tiger held the dog's head on his knees. Moki opened his eyes and struggled to get up.

Arcadie inspected the cut on Moki's head. "The bullet just grazed him. He'll be all right. With two doctors, he'll probably get well twice as fast."

Willie Tiger and Josh grinned in relief. They lifted the dog into the wagon and let him ride in comfort.

The following days passed slowly, dragging out in agonizing tension. The sun rose red and set red. The sand pulled at the wagon wheels. By midafternoon the horses hardly moved faster than the ox. Penny felt the heat more than the others. Willie Tiger and Josh began to take turns driving the wagon.

"We're going to be so tuckered out that we'll be easy pickin's for those two-legged buzzards," Eben said when they stopped for the night. "Maybe we should ambush them and get it over with."

Penny nearly dropped the pot she had taken from the wagon. "Eben Bramlett!"

The others stared.

"Not the kind of ambush they're planning for us," Eben replied. "What if we let the wagon go on ahead? We can spread out and get the drop on them when they come past. Then we can kind of arrest them ourselves."

"Arrest Zack's gang?" Arcadie's eyebrows raised and his mustache shook. "You got nerve, Eben Bramlett!"

"It'll be a fight either way," Eben replied. "And I'm not ancy for my folk to start in killin' if we can find another way to settle the matter."

Penny nodded, relief evident in her face. "I knew the Lord would show us a way."

Arcadie took a deep breath. "It might work. It'd have to work on the first try, or else. I'll ride out tonight and make sure they're still behind us. I wouldn't want to send Miz Penny and the boys right into their hands."

"We're staying with you two," Josh insisted.

"They certainly are," Penny agreed. "You'll need every hand to pull that off. I'll be all right with Ornery and Moki."

Reluctantly, Eben gave his consent. The wagon would have to keep moving to lure the riders into the trap.

Arcadie slipped out into the night. Hours later he returned, cautiously calling before stepping into sight. "They're about a mile back, still together. They're in no hurry. I reckon they do consider us easy pickin's."

"Tomorrow'll be proof one way or the other," Eben said soberly.

Josh didn't know how the others slept, but he felt like his eyelids had been stripped off. He stared unseeingly at the starlit sky. Dawn found him gritty-eyed and tense.

Arcadie tied the horses to long ropes and knotted the ends to the back of the wagon. The horses could move along with plenty of range, as if they were still being ridden. The men and boys got in the wagon. Penny got Ornery moving, and the wagon crunched across the rough ground.

About a mile down the trail, they approached scattered clumps of blackjack and turkey oak. "There." Eben pointed ahead. Quickly, he indicated that each would take a different stand, to catch the gang in a crossfire if needed. They nodded and gathered up their weapons. Josh saw Eben fold his bullwhip, and he reached for his own. Each leaped from the wagon seat after passing the clump, leaving no telltale tracks.

Once in concealment, Josh couldn't see the others. He stood the whip upright beside him and nervously cradled his rifle. The creaking of the wagon faded. Josh hadn't counted on the quiet. It crowded around him, cutting him off from everything he knew to be good.

When he heard the riders approaching, he felt more relief than fear. The voices drifted through the stillness, seeming closer than they really were. Josh's finger tightened on the trigger, but he forced himself to wait for his father.

The creaking of saddles grew into drumbeats. Josh took a deep breath.

"Stop right there." Eben stepped into the trail.

"I wouldn't, Zack."

Zack swung around to see Arcadie behind them, rifle ready. Josh stepped out from the right and saw Willie Tiger emerge on the left.

"Drop your weapons." Eben's voice was commanding.

Zack glared. "You two-bit crackers," he yelled and went for his gun.

Arcadie's rifle roared, and the whip cracked. The gun spun out of Zack's hand, and one of the other men fell heavily to the ground. The others held their hands up slowly.

"Keep 'em up," Arcadie shouted. "Up, Zack!"

The hands went into the air hesitantly, as the men stared in disbelief. Josh and Willie Tiger collected the guns quickly.

"Josh, Willie Tiger. Unload those guns and scatter the ammunition," Eben said. "Then fling the guns into the brush."

The boys obeyed quickly.

"Now get down," he told the riders.

They swung out of their saddles slowly, eyeing the whip. Arcadie swung into one of the saddles and took the reins of the other horses.

"You're not taking our horses!" one of the men cried out in anger. "It's four days to Punta Rassa! And Shorty's hurt!"

"I just winged him," Arcadie said coolly, inspecting the man who lay clutching his sleeve. "He'll live."

"We're not horse thieves," Eben said. "We'll let the horses loose tomorrow. I'm sure you'll catch them eventually. And I wouldn't leave anybody weaponless out here. You can find your guns and your shells if you look hard enough."

"If I wuz you," Arcadie said menacingly, leveling his rifle at Zack, "I'd head for the Islands and stay there. You'll find it a mite safer."

Zack sputtered as Eben and the boys swung up on the horses. They rode away, leaving him standing in the dust.

They caught up with Penny easily. She stopped Ornery and ran back to Eben. He swung her up before him, laughing. "We did it, Penny! We actually did it!"

Arcadie slapped his hat on his leg. "Thought I'd be the first to drop when you stepped out carrying that measly bullwhip. Who would've thought you could face down Zack with a whip!"

"Why did you, Pa?"

"If I'd stepped out with a rifle, they'd have drawn down right then and there. They didn't believe the whip either. It gave the rest of you a chance to corral them before everything busted loose."

Arcadie nodded. "That it did. But I'm not sure I'd 'a done it myself."

Josh felt a flush of pride. "Pa can knock a coon out of a live oak 'fore you can blink an eye."

"And it's a good thing too," Penny said, half-scolding. "Now put me back in the wagon. I still don't trust that gang of cutthroats, Eben. Let's put some miles between us and them."

Chapter Fourteen
All Trails Lead Home

The next day they released the horses. Josh and Willie Tiger ran them west, cracking the whips over their heads.

"Don't make it too easy," Arcadie called after them. "I shore don't want to see Zack again anytime soon!"

"Well, what now?" Eben asked when they returned. "Home is northeast for us, but what about you, Willie Tiger? The Big Cypress Swamp is south. That's where you'll find your people."

"You can't let him go off alone," Penny gasped. "Not in that kind of country! And with those blackguards still out there!"

"You can make your home with us, Willie," Eben said. "You know you're part of our family now."

Willie Tiger nodded. "I understand. And I thank you. But my grandfather had a dream. I'd like to see that at least part of it comes true."

"I'll take him."

Josh wheeled around. Arcadie cleared his throat and looked at Willie Tiger. "That is," he said gruffly, "if it's okay with Willie."

"Yes," Willie said with a trace of Daniel's dignity. "I will ride with you, Arcadie."

"Well," Eben said, "that's right fine. I'll give you what gold you both can carry, and the rest of your share will stay in the trunk until you come for it. Fair enough?"

"Okay with me." Arcadie shook Eben's hand. "You running another herd next spring?"

"As sure as there's yellowhammers in the scrub," Eben replied cheerfully. "You gonna be there?"

"I'll be there."

"So will I, Eben Bramlett," Willie Tiger said. He whistled to Moki and knelt beside him. He rubbed the dog as Josh had done and carefully inspected the slight graze on his head.

"I'm afraid Moki cannot travel right now," he said solemnly. "He looks worse."

Josh blinked and started to protest. "Why, he ate every bit of my jerky this morning. If that dog's sick, I'll—"

He saw the broad grins on Eben's and Arcadie's faces and stammered helplessly. Finally he got out, "I'll take good care of him, Willie Tiger. I promise."

He and his parents stood beside the wagon and watched as Willie Tiger and Arcadie rode south. Josh was surprised to find them disappearing in a blur of tears.

"I wish I'd had time to make biscuits." Penny turned away, busily fastening down canvas that was already tied tightly. "And you should've ridden with them for a while. Just until you could tell they were safe."

"Penny." Eben put his arms around her. "They'll be back in the spring. They'll be all right."

She sniffed. "I know."

Moki whined softly, staring out into the brush. Josh hugged him. "It's okay, boy. Let's go home."

Ornery picked up his pace as if he understood the words. They moved along right smartly, for the ox. Eben drove and Penny sat beside him. Josh rode ahead on Midnight, with Moki loping along at his heels.

"You know something, Penny?" Eben said thoughtfully.

"What, Eben?"

"Remember how green the grass was along the river? Remember the turkey and venison and soft-shelled turtle? And the quail and dove?"

Penny began to smile.

"I've been thinking. We could use some of the money to buy that land. It'd be ours, to keep. And Josh's, later on. We could build a cabin up near the trees, and put the holding pens down by the river." Eben's eyes began to gleam. "Can't you just see it, Penny? There'd be water for your orange trees. We could plant them up on the hills where they could get plenty of sun. What do you think, Pen?"

He turned to look at his wife. She tucked her arm under his and leaned against his shoulder. "It sounds just beautiful, Eben. Just beautiful."